Erotic Encounters

14 Days of Foreplay

By

Cheryl Duffy

First Printing: 2019

ISBN: 978-0-9963197-6-8

Epoch Publishing

Contents

INTRODUCTION

As a Divorce Recovery Coach, many clients have highlighted that their relationship has been impacted through the loss of intimacy or impacted by infidelity.

This book contains explicit sexual content depicted as 14 short erotic stories intended for couples who want to reconnect and spice up their sex life so they can reignite the passion and possibly avoid ending in Divorce.

Read a story alone or together prior to a night of passion to heighten the pleasure and ecstasy so you're begging for more!

Try to restrain your desire to the end of each story if you can.

1 EROTIC ENCOUNTERS WITH A COWBOY

1.1 TAMING THE BEAST

Susie walked into the saloon, a very self-assured woman, oozing confidence and sexual allure. She walked up to the bar and ordered a Bacardi and Coke in a short glass, no ice, then sat down on a stool to survey the talent. Susie had never been to a bar that had a mechanical bull and thought it would be fun to watch the competition between man and machine.

As the punters started to arrive, Susie assessed which ones may give the bull a run for its money. The local cowboys, used to taming the wild beasts on their ranches thought the mechanical bull should be easy to conquer. A tall blonde man, in his late 30's, walked up to the bar. He certainly noticed Susie as a new patron and started to admire her lean, athletic body. Her jeans were skin tight, hugging her hips and sitting low on her waist. Her white t-shirt was taut across her plentiful chest, outlining her rounded pert breasts. Her knee high boots were made of fine cow hide, with heels that accentuated the length of her legs that seemed to go on forever. With luscious long brown hair and beautiful blue eyes, Susie is a sight to behold. The blonde cowboy introduced himself as Mike and offered to buy Susie a drink which she accepted. As they sat chatting Susie couldn't help being distracted by Mike's physique. He had a muscular body, strong shoulders, and arms that had protruding veins down the forearms which she imagined bulging as he held onto the rope to dominate a bull into submission. Mike had chiselled features, strong jaw and cheek bones with blue eyes that pierced through to her very soul. As he smiled, the flash of white teeth, lit up his face, softening his rugged features and unveiling a vulnerable side.

They chatted for a while until the commentator boomed in a big voice that the competition to stay on the mechanical bull the longest would be starting in 5 minutes. Mike and Susie decided to move closer to the action, collecting their drinks and sitting at a ringside table. There were quite a few people gathering around, mostly men cheering their mates on to enter the competition. The winner who stays on the bull the longest gets to go into the next round the following night, to compete for a $500 prize.

Mike, full of confidence, tells Susie he is going to enter. Susie feels her excitement swell as she imagines him riding the bull clenching with his knees to stay on, rising and falling to the pulsating rhythm of the mechanical beast. As Mike goes to enlist, Susie surveys Mike's competitors and notices that there are 3 other men who are up for the challenge. They vary in age and physique, one man in his late 40's who has certainly weathered over the years from living on the land, rustling herds of cattle. Another man, very young, is only about 22 years old, tall and skinny. The last man, short and stocky has a lot of arrogance, thinking he is going to wipe his competitors out and become the victor. Susie feels confident Mike has a great chance to win.

The bell sounds and all four men line up outside the ring raring to take on the mechanical bull. The young skinny man eagerly yells out he wants to go first and leaps over the ring to get the competition started. He climbs onto the bull which is solid and still as though luring the boy into a false sense of ease. The boy gets into position and the commentator flicks the switch. The bull starts to move slowly rearing up and down and side to side in a gentle motion. The boy is holding on tight and smiling with quiet confidence. The bull speeds up thrusting the boy up and down, making it more difficult to hold on as he slides up and down the saddle. It isn't long before the boy is being whipped sideways, loses his balance and topples off the bull. Disappointed, the boy walks to the edge of the ring and jumps over. The commentator announces that the boy managed to stay on the bull for 26 seconds and calls up the next brave man. The short stocky guy struts over to the bull and climbs up, positioning himself for maximum duration. The bull starts to lunge and buck, the short guy clings on for dear life but struggles to stay on. His legs are not long enough to cling onto the belly of the bull and sure enough he gets thrown across the ring after 15 seconds. Ego bruised, the short guy moves out of the ring quickly, disappointed with his efforts.

The seasoned cowboy steps up with assurance that his longevity and experience in the business will bring him success. The bull starts to move faster and faster, going up and down and side to side trying to throw off the experienced cowboy, to no avail. His thighs are clinging onto the bull as he rides the bull confidently. The speed increases and the twisting to the side jerks him sharply but the cowboy continues to remain on the bull. The crowd cheers on impressed with the older cowboy's efforts. It is 3 minutes and 10 seconds and the cowboy is struggling to hold on. The final pulsating lunges throw the cowboy over the front of the bull, he lands hard on his back. Standing up, he holds his lower back and limps out of the ring, the crowd is cheering loudly impressed with his efforts. It's Mike's turn and Susie gets butterflies and cheers him on. He saunters over to the bull confidently and slides on with a dominance of ownership over the beast. The bull starts to gyrate side to side and up and down trying to throw Mike off. Mike rides the bull as though they are one, moving to the same rhythm. Susie notices how strong and muscular his thighs are, gripping the bull underneath his writhing body. The muscles in Mike's arms are bulging as he holds onto the rope, restraining the bull's power. The thrusting of Mike's body in rhythmic movement with the bull has Susie excited as she imagines him taking control of her body, guiding it through the throes of passion. The bull moves faster and faster, bucking harder and harder trying to eject Mike from its back. The sweat starts to roll down Mike's chest and his shirt clings to his body emphasising the abs locked on in battle with the bull. Mike's hips are thrust forward with every lunge of the bull, his jeans strain against his groin as he too grows with the excitement of dominating the beast. The focus and determination on Mike's face shows he is taking the competition seriously and has managed to stay on the bull 2 minutes and 55 seconds. The crowd goes wild as he passes the 3-minute mark, inching closer to the lead. Susie jumps up and starts cheering for Mike to stay strong and hold on. Mike continues to be thrust harder and harder, as he is twisted from side to side, jerking his body violently as he struggles to hold on. The crowd lets out a huge cheer when the clock reaches 3 minutes 11 seconds as he surpasses his competitor putting him in the lead. He stays on a further 10 seconds before being thrown off the back of the bull. The commentator announces Mike as the winner and urges Mike to jump back onto the bull for a photo opportunity. Mike beckons Susie to join him and she sits in front as he straddles the bull behind her. The bull is activated slowly to celebrate Mike's victory. Mike puts his strong arms around Susie to hold her in place so she doesn't fall off, his body pins her tighter to the bull securing her. Susie feels Mike's strong body lunging forward and up, she feels shivers go up her spine as he does his victory ride over the bull and her. He knows that she is relaxing her body back into his and letting his rhythm with the bull carry them both through the waves of sexual tension. He rests his hands on the top of her thighs as they both pulsate with the rhythm whilst the crowd goes wild and cheers them on.

Susie and Mike walk out of the saloon triumphant, adrenaline pumping, excited about the victory. Mike takes hold of Susie's hand and leads her to his pickup truck. He opens the door for her, as she goes to climb in he grabs her, spinning her to face him and kisses her passionately yet gently holding her cheek with his hand. Susie feels her loins tingle with excitement and her breath escapes her as she is taken off guard. She responds to his kiss and puts her hand to his chest feeling his heart pounding furiously. She wants him as much as he wants her and they feverishly kiss, passionately feeling each other's bodies as though exploring for the first time. Susie knows this is happening far too quickly but is carried away by his overpowering passion, as he pushes his groin into her, pinning her to the car. Susie becomes more breathless as she feels her womanhood respond and become moist with anticipation. She lets out a groan, Mike kisses her harder and caresses her breasts through her clothing, her nipples are erect, they beg for his touch. Mike pulls her T-Shirt out from her jeans and lifts it high to show her lace see through bra displaying her smooth pert breasts which are hardened with excitement. He unfastens her bra freeing her to the elements. He lifts her t-shirt and bra off over her head and the cool breeze washes over her, her nipples harden further with anticipation. He slowly starts to flick his tongue over her left nipple and she groans with pleasure. He sucks softly stretching the nipple

11

sending tingling sensations over her body. His left hand caresses her right nipple ever so softly gliding across backwards and forwards flicking the nipple as it grows harder and harder to his touch. Susie reaches for his pants, unbuckling his belt and easing the zipper down, releasing his manhood which jumps out like a jack in the box eager to reach her searching hand. She glides her soft small hand along his shaft sending tingles to the very tip. Susie lowers herself down and slowly flicks the head with her tongue increasing the saliva released to lubricate the movement. She slowly glides his member into her mouth and closes her lips around him sucking tighter and tighter gliding up and down his shaft pushing him further into her mouth. She cups his sack in her hand and slowly massages it and she feels him pulsate in her mouth growing deeper and deeper.

Mike pulls Susie up wanting to savour the love making longer and lays her across the front bench seat. Her breasts are still hard as he unzips her jeans and pulls them down to her ankles and off the bottom of her feet. Her lace panties show the outline of her womanhood, he can smell her excitement as she moistens further, anticipating his entry. He slowly pulls her panties down over her thighs and off completely leaving her naked sprawled across his front seat. Susie feels extremely vulnerable in this position yet

12

supercharged with excitement. He slowly parts her legs to gain access to her flower and flicks his tongue on her clitoris which drives her wild. He licks her ravenously, sucking at her clitoris and making her groan as she grabs hold of his head with both hands to guide him. He is rock hard at seeing the excitement he is creating in Susie, he pulls her up to her feet turning her around and bending her over the front seat. Mike, still standing outside of the truck, has her soft bottom bent over in front of him and Susie arching her back pushes herself back onto him so he can gain entry, her love juices leaking to enable him to glide into her with ease. He pushes his full length into her and she groans with pleasure as he fills her to capacity, pulsating slowly gliding in and out. He holds her hips and pushes deeper into her and she lets out a cry of passion beckoning him to take her. Mike thrusts harder and harder as though taming the mechanical bull, holding her in place and riding her with determination and passion. His thrusts quicken and he seems to be getting closer to climax when Susie beckons him to hold on so they can cum together. She pushes him back so he can withdraw and turns onto her back, puts her feet onto his shoulders pushing into him and beckoning him to re-enter. He pulls her hips to the edge of the seat to gain maximum entry, as he thrusts into her she lets out a groan of passion. Mike uses his thumb to massage Susie's clitoris and feels her love canal tighten around him. Susie writhes in passion and thrusts into him sending him deeper. They are both groaning and writhing in passion until both their bodies convulse and shudder in climax as they slump into a heap, totally spent, panting breathlessly.

Mike slowly helps Suzie up, collecting her strewn clothes from outside the car, so that she can get dressed. He pulls up his jeans and buckles his belt as Susie awkwardly dresses herself, feeling a shyness that moments earlier had escaped her whilst in the throes of passion. Mike says "I hope you will return for the rematch tomorrow night." Susie nodded not knowing if he meant the mechanical bull competition or their love making. Both reached out and kissed one another softly and tenderly, with their eyes lingering, as they started to go their own way.

Susie reached home, removed all her clothes and jumped into the shower. Washing away the scent of the cowboy she relived the events of the night in her mind. Her body remembered and started to respond to her own soft touch of the silky soap gliding over her body and passing over her erect nipples as the warm water sprayed hard onto her breasts. Thoughts of Mike's strong body holding her and caressing every inch of her body sent shivers up her spine. She turned and the shower flowed down her back trickling between her buttocks. Susie turned the water off and reached for her bathrobe. She wrapped it around her body giving her a warm, safe feeling as she lay on her bed slipping into a deep sleep, reminiscing about the encounter she had with Mike the cowboy and how she couldn't wait to see him the next night.

1.2 VICTORY RIDE

The next night Susie was intent on dressing very sexy, almost to present herself as the prize to Mike, who she was sure would win the mechanical bull contest. Her black lingerie, which consisted of a lacy push up bra and G-string, which left nothing to the imagination, she laid out on her bed. Donning herself in the lingerie she then gingerly pulled on black suspender stockings. Clipping them into place she paraded in front of the mirror admiring herself and feeling super confident with her sexual prowess. The lingerie was then overlaid with a short black dress which clung to her slender figure exposing her cleavage. Ready, she set out to cheer on her cowboy!

Susie arrived at the saloon and walked in confidently seeing heads turn as she made her presence felt. Mike was at the bar with his back to her, she sauntered up behind him and softly touched his arm. He swung around and gasped at her beauty, he kissed her softly on the lips and touched her cheek rubbing his thumb across her smooth skin. He ordered her a drink remembering, Bacardi and Coke, short glass, no ice. She was impressed! Susie asked him if he was ready for the wild ride tonight, now it was Mike's turn to wonder if she meant the mechanical bull or their love making afterwards. The commentator announced 5 minutes till the start of the contest so Mike and Susie headed over towards the arena to get a table and survey the competitors. There were 3 new competitors and Mike was announced as the reigning champion. The other competitors consisted of a young mate of last night's 22-year-old competitor, who was very cocky, thinking he was going to do a better job than his mate. He too was a slip of a boy but most energetic. The next competitor was a tall dark handsome fellow who must have been in his 40's with a wife in tow egging him on to make her proud. The final competitor was another slip of a boy aged about 18 and quietly reserved. The commentator called up the eager 22-year old's mate as the first contestant. He climbed up onto the bull, whoop whooping to his mates in the crowd, who were cheering him on holding up their glasses of beer toasting his efforts. The bull started to move slowly up and down and side to side, the boy confidently rode it with ease. The bucking increased and the twists and turns had him struggling to stay seated until suddenly after 1minute and 40 seconds he was thrown off to the side, with his mates cheering loudly as he had surpassed his mate from the night before. Next was the 40-year-old married man who swaggered into the arena giving his wife a wink, as she excitedly blew him a kiss. The bull swung into action and the married man clung on confidently with his thighs as though he had been doing this for years. The crowd were cheering as he surpassed the youngster's time, he seemed to be handling the bull with ease thrusting his body to the rhythm of the bull mastering its moves. The speed intensified, the bucking jerked him up and down with sharp turns to the left and right until he couldn't hold on any longer and was thrown off swiftly at 2 minutes and 53 seconds. His wife was so proud of him, she threw her arms around his neck and kissed him as though he was the only cowboy alive. Next the other slip of a boy was ushered up and everyone thought, like his predecessors, he wouldn't last very long. He jumped onto the bull and wriggled into a comfortable position. The bull tried to flick off the lightweight but he clung on with determination, managing to stay on for 3 minutes and 15 seconds, exceeding Mike's time of the night before. As the lightweight got up off the floor his hat fell off, revealing that he was in fact a young girl, with long locks and a determined spirit. Everyone was shocked and Susie was quietly proud that this young girl outstripped the cowboys and currently led the competition. Mike felt a sudden surge of panic, what if this slip of a girl beats him in front of Susie and his fellow cowboys. Susie leaned in close to him, whispered "I know you can do this" and kissed him passionately. His adrenaline soared through his veins and he climbed onto the bull. He knew he had to beat his time of last night, he focused intently, with sheer determination to show Susie he was the strong cowboy he demonstrated he was last night, both on and off the bull! He took a last look at Susie, who looked stunning, giving him the rush of testosterone he needed to take charge of the bull. The jerking intensified, lurching up and down, sharply left to right, sweat pouring down his back and his forehead. Susie watched on, excited at the rhythmic movements he was mastering over the bull and thinking he would be mastering his moves on her later. The time was getting closer to the 3-minute mark and the crowd was going wild. Mike only had to hold on for another 16 seconds to become the overall champion, not only winning $500 but more importantly impressing Susie. The crowd started to count the seconds chanting them loudly 10, 11, 12, 13, 14, 15, with a fevered pitch then screamed 16 to alert Mike he was the winner. Mike continued to hold on until 3 minutes 22 seconds then was thrown off, soaked with sweat lying in a heap on the floor of the arena. Susie ran across to him, knelt beside him, concerned that he was hurt, but he grabbed her face and kissed her passionately and the crowd went wild. The commentator was shouting that Mike was the champion, handed him the winning envelope and a well-earned beer. Mike downed the whole beer then said to Susie "let's get out of here". He took her by the hand and ushered her to his truck.

As they drove off, Susie wondered where they were going. They pulled onto a long drive which meandered for a few kilometres down a track until a homestead could be seen in the distance. He pulled up outside the house and opened the door for Susie to enter. The homestead was quaint. Mike suggested that Susie pour them a drink from the bar whilst he took a shower. Susie obliged and could see that Mike had left the door ajar so she could see his tanned, tall, muscular body dripping as he dried himself and wrapped the towel around his waist. Drinks ready, Susie decided to put on a show of her own, she slipped out of her dress only leaving her sexy lingerie, stockings and stilettos on. Picking up the drinks Susie pushed the door to Mike's bedroom open and walked in half undressed, this took him by surprise. They stood admiring each other's bodies, until Susie handed Mike his drink saying "I think you're going to need this!" Susie walked over to the bedside table and put her drink down, she then walked back to Mike who had gulped his drink and was almost quivering. It was evident who had the power at this moment and Susie was enjoying watching Mike squirm. She licked her finger and slowly ran circles around Mike's nipple, which made it go erect with excitement. She slowly glided her fingernails down his torso to his belly and Mike's manhood started to respond to her touch. Susie softly pushed Mike backwards so that he lost his balance and fell onto the bed. Mike was sitting on the edge of the bed when Susie pushed his chest backwards telling him to relax and lie down. Susie bent down between his legs and ran her finger nails softly up and down his thighs. Mike continued to grow with the anticipation of Susie's next move, he lay with his hands under his head which accentuated his muscular arms and torso. Susie started to blow hot breath softly around Mike's genitals without touching him which continued to arouse him. She starts to glide her tongue along the shaft, stopping to deposit soft kisses along the way to the head, where she lets her tongue explore. Dribbling saliva onto the head and pushing it around in circles with her tongue made Mike's member move involuntarily as if it was trying to reach out to meet Susie's every touch. Kissing softly back down the shaft she teases him by sucking his soft skin sack and sucking it into her mouth. With a playful nibble he jumps, she puts her hand on his belly to push him back down. He can feel the smirk on her face as she takes his member into her mouth and glides it softly deeper. She tightens her mouth around him and glides up and down making him groan and totally relax under her control. Susie stands up and straddles Mike on the bed, he thinks she looks like a dominatrix in her black lingerie. Holding his arms in place with her hands so he can't escape, she rubs herself against his chest and he feels the lace tickling his skin. She sits up, slowly undoing her bra and releasing her breasts which are erect with excitement. Mike immediately sits bolt upright cupping her breasts and taking her nipple into his mouth, sucking it hard which makes Susie arch her back and moan with passion. She can feel Mike's hardness underneath her and starts to feel her love juices beckon his entry. Mike pushes her panties aside and moves his fingers into her, feeling soft warm juices trickle down his hand. Her breathing starts to increase as Mike replaces his fingers with his manhood, pushing deep inside her as she rides him like the mechanical bull, arching her back and moaning in waves of passion. Mike increases the momentum, thrusting deeper and deeper while caressing her breasts with his hands. Susie starts to caress her clitoris which makes her tighten around Mike's member. Neither want this to end too quickly. Mike withdraws from Susie, rolls her onto her back with her knees apart so he can gain access with his mouth. He softly flicks her clitoris with his tongue which makes Susie groan with pleasure. The tongue travels down Susie's beckoning lips gliding with ease and enters her. Mike pushes himself forward and Susie groans, grabbing hold of his head bringing him closer to her. Mike starts to lick and suck her clitoris sending waves of passion through Susie's body. Mike stands up and guides Susie onto her knees bent over before him. He slowly pushes his rod deep into her and she gasps with delight. Mike starts to rhythmically increase the pace holding her hips still and squeezing them tightly. Their breathing and groaning starts to increase, Susie reaches down to caress her clitoris and she moans further. Mike lubricates his thumb in his mouth then pushes it into Susie's bottom, she lets out a cry feeling the pleasure and pain simultaneously but pushes back into him whilst increasing the rubbing of her own clitoris and Mike increasing his thrusts. He can feel Susie start to tighten, then all of a sudden her body convulses as she cries out loudly exploding with intensity. Mike pumps harder and faster, he too shudders as waves of convulsion grip his body and he groans loudly. They both twitch with the last drops of energy they have and fall onto the bed with Mike laying his heavy body on top of hers. They are both panting breathlessly, Susie puts her arms above her head and Mike lays his on top of hers, grasping her hands with their fingers entwined. They lie as one, fully spent, as their sweat melds them. Revived and feeling sleepy Mike lifts himself off of Susie and takes her by the hand, Susie removes her lingerie, they both climb into his bed naked and Mike spoons Susie wrapping his arms around her holding her close. They drift off to sleep feeling content that they have found each other.

1.3   TETHERED BY THE RIVER

Susie awakens to find herself alone in the bed, at first bewildered as to where she was, but suddenly remembers Mike and the amazing love making the night before. She climbs out of bed and pulls on Mike's shirt from last night, she walks out to the kitchen where she finds Mike making breakfast. Susie sits on the stool opposite him and asks how she can help; Mike tells her to relax pouring her a cup of coffee. They both smile at one another feeling comfortable in each other's presence. Mike asks Susie if she feels like going for a ride on horseback to a river nearby, and Susie exclaims that that sounds like fun.

After breakfast Susie heads home to shower and put on some appropriate clothes for horse riding. On her return, they saddle up and start their journey into the vast countryside as though they are the only humans alive. They reach the river and it certainly is a pretty spot, some shaded trees to tie up the horses and soft green grass for them to sit on to take in the view. It is extremely hot and they decide it would be great to go for a swim in the river. They both strip off all their clothes and jump into the water. After a short time of swimming around to cool off, they find their bodies being pulled closer together, almost via an invisible magnet. They hold each other and start kissing softly then more and more passionately. Susie wraps her legs around Mike's waist and he soon gains entry to her. Their breath becomes more laboured; they feel the water engulf their naked bodies as they are connected as one. They decide to get out of the water to continue their love making, Mike grabs the rope off his saddle and takes Suzie's hand guiding her to the shaded tree. He gets Susie to stand with her back to the tree, feet apart and hands behind her back as he ties her naked to the tree. He picks up a small twig which has leaves on it and uses this to glide over Susie's body softly tickling her, making her squirm. He glides the leaves across her nipples, up her thighs and between her legs, driving her wild. He can see that her excitement at being restrained is making her love juices flow, preparing her to enable his ease of entry. Mike bends down on his knees to be under Susie and parts her lips with his fingers, flicking her clitoris with his tongue. Susie is breathing heavily and groaning at his tender touch. Mike feels his member growing as it responds to Susie's cries of passion, he stands up and pushes it against Susie who is still restrained to the tree. He bends his knees to lower his height so he can enter Susie, she lets out a cry as he pushes into her. He cups her face in his hands and kisses her passionately as she responds hungrily. He then holds onto her hips and continues to thrust up into her, she writhes unable to move as she is still tethered to the tree under his power to do whatever he likes. In this vulnerable position being unable to escape and naked to the elements, makes Susie so excited so it isn't long before she can feel her body shudder with climax. Mike pumps harder and harder groaning louder and holding Susie tight as he feels his power over her vulnerable body. As he cums, Mike yells out loudly in passion. He cums with such force shuddering into her body, jerking the last drops of himself, feeling totally exhausted.

Mike unties Susie and they both slump into each other's embrace, on the soft green grass. Susie feels content, she sighs thinking she has found her cowboy to ride off into the sunset.

2 EROTIC ENCOUNTERS WITH A SLAVE

2.1 SLAVE ADONIS

At the local market I ponder around the wares that are on sale, I wander through the narrow corridors of stalls until I come to an open area where they are selling men, to be sex slaves for a week, you hire them to do as you please before returning them. I see there are about 20 men to choose from, mostly Asian, with taut Bruce lee abs from martial arts training. I then catch the eye of a blonde Adonis, who stands 6"3 with the body of an angel, rock hard thighs, defined hips, soft belly and a throbbing member just awaiting my tender touch. His blue eyes penetrate my soul and there is a connection, I just know I have to have him. The problem is that the bidding has started and the blonde number 29042016 has already caught the attention of a middle eastern man, who wants to use the blonde as part of the entertainment in his palace to pleasure his many wives, the bidding is high…. too hard for me to compete.

I try to keep up with the bidding, I must have this Adonis to satisfy my own pleasures. I feel a deep yearning to have this man inside me, to take me as his own and mark me as his territory.... never to be touched by another. I see in his eyes that he hopes I can secure the final bid; my body already feels the electrifying intensity between us. Bidders are allowed to touch and inspect the prize as the bidding continues. I wander over, my nipples are already erect with anticipation of his mouth and tongue encircling them, the skin on my back fires up like an electric fence and shivers with the anticipation of his hands rubbing oil into my back and down to my bottom. My thighs tingle as love juice has already started to dribble down my legs, ready to invite this man to my very sacred centre.

I can see that his manhood is reacting to my body's response, it grows in length, girth and is standing to attention. He is shackled with his hands behind his back and his ankles tethered to avoid him running away from slavery, but this man isn't going anywhere, even if he was unshackled as he is entranced by the prospects of the love making he could experience under my control and orders. I softly touch his chest, flicking his nipples and gliding my fingernails down his stomach, accidentally touching his member as I hover over his belly button. His eyes meet mine and we melt into one another's hearts. As I say to myself that this man must be mine, the Middle Eastern man moves in to take a closer look at the prize. He needs to see if the Adonis will satisfy his numerous wives, since he has struggled to maintain their constant desires for his seduction. This man is also aged 43 like the Adonis, and he eyes up his competition to fulfil his wives' desires. He touches the biceps of the Adonis to see if he is strong and fit, he checks the teeth of the Adonis to see if they are healthy, he makes the Adonis bend over to see if he has a taught bottom, which he imagines thrusting into his wives' bodies. This man doesn't realise how badly I want the Adonis and the seller, knowing both parties want him, hands the power to the Adonis to choose.

Now there is a power shift from between me and the Middle Eastern man to the Adonis. He revels in the delight of demonstrating his skills. He decides to show us how he can lick and suck the flesh of a watermelon displaying the skills he would endure for the woman he desires. He pushes his tongue deep into the melon feeling the juice slide down his chin, he slurps the juices down his throat enjoying the sweet taste. He then uses his manhood to penetrate deep into the watermelon, showing the sheer thrusting power he possesses to take a woman with force and hold her so tightly in place that she cannot escape. I could hardly contain my laboured breath as I watched the Adonis demonstrate his manly force, knowing that he would not only satisfy me, but connect with me, mind body and soul as our energies collide. The Middle Eastern man now starts to become concerned that his wives may enjoy this Adonis more than him. He decides to choose an Asian man who is not as well-endowed as himself knowing full well that his wives would be pleasured, but would still long for him as their favourite lover.

The Adonis looks at me as I smile victoriously, knowing I have won, I take his hand......

2.2 WINNER

Just as I take the Adonis's hand a shriek comes from the crowd, an Asian lady doubles my bid. I turn to the auctioneer to plead, I won the auction fair and square and the Adonis is my prize. The auctioneer, a shrewd business man, knows nothing about being fair. He knows how much money he can make by selling off the slave like a piece of meat today, and have him returned unspoiled the following week to go thru the same ritual again and again. He knows he has a fine specimen in this blonde, but the auctioneer is not driven by money alone as he also has a deep desire to see the sexual skills displayed between the purchaser and the prize. The auctioneer orders the slave to release my hand and declares that the price will be halfway between my bid and the Asian lady's bid. The clincher is, however, that each us women has to tantalise the Adonis through our sexual skills thus enabling him to choose who is worthy. This is a cruel blow to have my prize stripped away from me, but as I want the Adonis so badly I agree to participate in this game of slave seduction. We are both ordered to disrobe and stand before the crowd which is growing as fast as the Adonis's member, which is on display being fully engorged with the anticipation of our seductive prowess.

The Asian lady is selected to go first; her sleek body is tiny without an ounce of fat. She must be in her 30's, still in her prime, and has what it takes to lure a man with her svelte build. She is very acrobatic with tight abs and strong thighs. She immediately lurches forward into a handstand before the Adonis, her back hard up against him, her legs splayed at each of his shoulders so he has her womanhood within striking range of his mouth. He can smell her musk and sees she wants him bad. He plunges his tongue hard and strong into her honeypot. She gasps with delight, almost teetering off balance, he wraps his arms around her thighs holding her tight in his grip so that he can devour her. She is unable to retreat from his advance. The Adonis sucks at her clitoris sending shivers up her thighs making her legs go weak like jelly. The constant barrage of licking, sucking and slurping her love juices can be heard from the crowd who go wild with excitement, they chant louder and louder for her to reach climax and with an explosive shriek her orgasm commences with such intensity it spurts love juice into the Adonis's eyes. With her thighs and bottom thrusting for that last wave of ecstasy, her body slumps into a heap and the Adonis wipes his mouth with his forearm. With that display I feel so hot and wet myself with the anticipation of connecting with the Adonis.........

2.3   THE CHALLENGE

My time has come to win over the Adonis. I know that the Asian acrobatic orgasm was a masterpiece in the eyes of the crowd, the auctioneer and the Adonis.......but he was still rock hard, obviously he himself was not satisfied by the Asian even though she had been. That was it, the key to me winning the Adonis was to please him, to satisfy him. This was not the norm for a male slave who was used to satisfying his owners who did not care about him or his desires. It was time to empower the slave in receipt of his own satisfaction with the hope that this would free him sexually and psychologically. This man had been forced to have sex with many women of all creeds, sizes and ages but never had any been tender enough to consider his needs.

I take the Adonis by the hand and kiss him tenderly with slow encircling flicks of my tongue which connect with his inner soul. The energy between us is electrifying, we can feel the heat between our bodies as we hold each other close. Our hearts beat to the same rhythm and our breathing increases in intensity. After I lovingly guide him onto all fours on the ground, I blindfold him.   His breath has increased in pace and his heart has started to pound harder as unknown and unseen activity will occur without notice.

With the sexual display witnessed with the Asian my own love juices had been flowing, I lay under the Adonis with my head facing up at his manhood and my womanhood under his face. He can't see it but can smell the scent of me as I insert two fingers into my womanhood to coat them with natural lubricant to be used on the Adonis to enter his body. I slowly remove my fingers from within myself feeling the juice run down their length. I slowly enter my fingers into his bottom easing softly so as not to hurt him, his body lunges with shock as neither did he expect nor see what was going to happen. I push my fingers to their full extent deep into the Adonis. As he groans with delight, I start to lick and salivate along the shaft of his member and feel it respond in my mouth. With his manhood fully in my mouth, I suck and lick around the head which drives the Adonis wild, while still repeatedly thrusting my fingers into his bottom. I wanted the Adonis to have a multitude of sensations. I then took my other hand and started caressing his manhood sliding up and down before thrusting my fingers into my womanhood to collect my natural lubricant and smearing it the length of his shaft. The Adonis could feel his manhood and his bottom being worked, I then sucked on his skin sack, repeatedly massaged it with my tongue while grinding my teeth over its tough texture. The crowd went wild seeing the Adonis moan and groan writhing under the trifecta of sensations pulsating through his body, his shaft, his sack and his bottom all being worked simultaneously and sending his nerve endings into overload. He could feel the crescendo of pressure as his bottom tightened, his manhood throbbed and he started to thrust uncontrollably until a fountain of his own love juice squirted onto my belly. He slumped down on me his heart pounding a million miles an hour......

2.4 VICTORY

The Adonis was heavy, a dead weight as he lay on top of me spent of sexual energy. The auctioneer ordered him to get up. The Adonis rose groggily to his feet, exhausted, still blindfolded to the senses of sight. I was ordered to remove his blindfold. I stood up, took the blindfold off and our eyes connected on another level. It was a deep connection, like our souls transforming into one energy. I softly kissed him and stroked his lovingly face. The auctioneer shouted "ENOUGH" and pushed me to aside. The Asian lady was on one side of the Adonis and me on the other. The auctioneer looked out to the crowd and engaged a roar of success that the slave seduction game was triumphant. The crowd responded with cheers as a new found market of entertainment had been unveiled. The auctioneer could see that the slave seduction could become a lucrative enterprise as the final phase of future slave transactions, with the opportunity to charge the crowd to see this entertainment. The crowd once again roared with excitement that they may be part of this experience again. The auctioneer requested that the Adonis choose a winner. He looked at both of us fleetingly then with loving eyes chose me. The auctioneer declared that I return the Adonis the next week for resale. I had mixed emotions, I was happy I had won him but felt sad knowing he wasn't mine indefinitely, that I would have to give him up after one week. I decided to push the sad thoughts to the back of my mind and revel in the pleasure I would have with the Adonis over the next week. Because I had pleasured him today and satisfied his desires, he looked at me with a new found gratitude. He had strong sense of how to pleasure me in return.

I took him by the hand and led him to my home which would also become his for the week. Until now he had always been ordered as to what sexual favours to complete, to be submissive or have the owner take advantage of his body. This time the Adonis felt an inner power had been released. I had unshackled him from a life of service and exposed him to a life where his desires were also important. The Adonis took charge, removing my clothing as I stood in anticipation of his next move. My breath started to labour as I caressed his taut body and let my hands glide, exploring every inch of his body, almost like taking a memory test so as to hold onto the feel, the responses, the pattern of desire that may develop as a new touch invoked new responses.

I knew the first encounter would be exploratory as we felt each other all over and connected at a higher level. His soft touch hovered above my skin making it tremble with anticipation. My touch was gliding my fingernails down his back, across his thighs and gently caressing his manhood as it grew in my hand. He reached down to my core which was already warm and wet, anticipating of his touch, as he pushed his fingers into me I groaned with pleasure. He massaged my G spot creating great pressure and pleasure. Meanwhile he flicked his tongue at my clitoris making it swell and long for a vigorous connection. My legs wrapped around his waist, he slowly lifted one of my legs to each of his shoulders, then thrust himself into me, both of us exerting a groan of pleasure. The thrusting intensified and soon I felt my body convulse and cling onto his manhood, not letting go, pulsating like in death throws. The wave of pleasure flowed over me repeatedly, crashing my body into the depths of climax. I couldn't catch my breath, my moans intensified until I fell, spent and unable to move, in a heap of exhaustion.

I looked up at the Adonis and we melted, emotionally converging into one.......

2.5   BOUND BY THE ADONIS

I awoke first, momentarily wondering where I was, the Adonis opened his eyes and I felt warm and secure in his presence. We both smiled, knowing we were truly safe in each other's arms. He lay there telling me about his life and the experiences that had affected him hard as he grew up. I couldn't help but think that our paths had crossed for a reason, as though the universe had plans that destined for us to be together. Whether that be me coming into the Adonis's life to help him heal or perhaps it was vice versa. We both certainly felt the connection, as though we had known each other for years, maybe even a thousand years in previous lives, reconnecting on each journey of our souls.

Our energies seem to electrify with each touch, as we both struggled to keep our hands off of one another. We start to stroke each other slowly, caressing, gliding our hands softly over every inch of each other's bodies. This process seems to be a ritual, connecting our energies to become one. The Adonis had spent a lot of his slave life shackled, used and abused as desired by former owners, unable to be free from the chains of slavery.

My own desire to be tied up and devoured, coupled with his desire to be unshackled and released to freedom took us to another level. The Adonis found some rope and cleared the kitchen table. The table was rectangular with four legs. Each leg to be used to anchor one of my limbs, to pin me onto the table allowing him to do whatever he desired, and me unable to protest. This would take an extreme amount of trust from me, in a man I had only known for such a short time, even though it felt like a lifetime. It excited me and scared me at the same time. What if things got out of hand? I'm putting myself in a very vulnerable position, unable to take back control, but I trusted the Adonis. I felt that he didn't just think of me as a pleasure source but had deeper feelings.

He stood me at one end of the table and bent me over, face down, spread my legs apart and attached them each to a table leg. Then he secured my arms above my head to the other two table legs. I could feel my womanhood tingle with anticipation and the love juices start to flow. The Adonis rubbed oil into my back with his strong hands, then taking his lubricated hands down my bottom and thighs. I could feel my breath quicken, my heart pound and my love juices intensify as the anticipation of his entry grew closer and closer. He placed a strong hand directly onto my back, as though to pin me in place, then his member entered me from behind filling the void to capacity. I let out a cry of pleasure as my womanhood clung onto him to ride through the event with pulsating waves. His thrusts sent shivers right up my spine and I felt he connected with me on an unknown level. He felt like he was a part of me, joining with me as one. My love for him had started to blossom, but how could that be, as he is not available to be mine. I needed to try to detach but this power or spell he had over me claimed me as his own. He thrust his full length in and out with driving force, I clenched the rope with each anticipated blow which rocked my world. I could feel the intensity increase and soon the crescendo of passion convulsed in the delights of climax, both of us moaning and groaning as our bodies entwined, mine would not release his member clutching him to stay, never to be released. We both fell in a heap, energies spent, with an aurora of calmness and peace as we lay together. His warm heavy body lying on mine, almost protecting and shielding me from another, to be forever his.

2.6 REPLENISHED

The Adonis unties my limbs from the table, he cradles me in his arms as if he is my saviour from the clutches of an abductor. I melt into his body feeling safe and protected. He lifts me and carries me to the bed, laying me down gently. He puts a cup of water to my lips telling me to drink. I guzzle the water to replenish the fluids I had lost. He then put a grape into his mouth and brought it across to my mouth, I bite off half and we share the fruits of our love making. He repeatedly fed me, like a mother bird, nurturing me to full strength. I could feel my energy start to recharge. The feel of his warm breath and his body so close to mine had started the vibrations of sensual desire. I sat up and lay the shoulders of the Adonis on the bed, I straddled him, pinning him down to endure my advances.

I caressed his shoulders with my fingertips circling then gliding down his chest. I leaned onto him taking his right nipple into my mouth and flicking it with my tongue, encircling it as it grew erect. I then sucked it hard which made him flinch. I moved across to the other nipple, which was already erect with anticipation of what was to come. I licked and stroked it with my tongue before once again sucking hard. I could feel his member start to harden against my thigh, I started to rub my thighs up and down his, very slowly, to savour the connection. With each movement ensuring that my nipples were freely gliding across the top of his chest and belly.

I kissed him passionately, feeling my love juices flow. My thighs started to moisten as the juice flowed down my legs in anticipation of his entry. I hovered above his erect appendage almost teasing it with the anticipation. I then suddenly sat on it, forcing its entry hard into me, resulting in us both gasping with delight. I then slowly glided my inner warmth ever so slowly along his shaft right to the tip before again slamming down hard, taking his full length inside me. This intensified our breathing, the torturous play of slow then fast, shocking the senses whilst trying to anticipate what the next move may be. I then pushed the Adonis's thighs open and lay between his legs taking the male stance, his member still inside me. I gyrated and thrust fast, driving him hard into me, still pinning his shoulders to the bed. He responded with thrusts that matched mine, we ensured the full length of him drove the whole way into me. The thrusting intensified, we could feel the tightening below as my womanhood clenched him tight convulsing into orgasm. The tight pressure around his member intensified the sensation for him and he exploded in me with a bellow of delight. I slumped onto his body, a dead weight, unable to move I almost defied his freedom to leave. We looked into each other's eyes and felt a softness and warmth that only love can bring....

42

Time is Drawing Near

I have had the Adonis imprisoned in my home for 5 days, not only like the sex slave I had won, but with a deep love for this man who seemed to penetrate my very soul. I only had him for another 2 days before he was due to return to the market to be rehired. I tried to prevent my tears welling up, I loved this man although he was not mine to be loved. I had opened my heart to him when I shouldn't have, as from the beginning he was never available to be mine. What was I thinking? Why did I put myself into this torturous situation where I would have to let him go? I started to feel myself panic! What could I do to keep him? Maybe I could take the Adonis far away but with his penalty for escape being death, we would be hunted down forever. No, I had to put those thoughts out of my head and trust that the universe would keep us together. I didn't want the next 2 days to be sad so decided to enjoy the time I had left with the Adonis.

I see he is asleep, lying on his side with his knees bent. I sidle up behind him taking on the same shape, spooning his body along mine. I feel his warmth radiate the entire length of my body and in his sleep his hand drops behind him falling onto my thigh. I take it in my hand and hold it tenderly. I then start to kiss him gently on his back with my moist soft lips. He stirs, he has felt my touch and responds, awakening from a deep sleep with his member erect and ready for action. I start to stroke it softly, up and down the shaft. He rolls over to face me and we kiss tenderly yet passionately. My womanhood starts to tingle with anticipation. I stroke his undercarriage, the soft sack of skin and perineum... a gentle touch. I push him onto his back, straddle him but deny entry at first to enable my flower to lubricate in preparedness. I wrap my legs around his waist still denying him entry, it drives him wild. I kiss him softly and my denial drives passion into his kiss to hasten my womanhood for readiness but I continue to deny. We embrace, thighs touching and me straddled around his waist with my womanhood dripping onto his member as though beckoning him to enter, but still I deny. The kissing becomes frantic, almost pleading for access, I continue to deny. I thrust my hand around his chest taking his nipple into my mouth and suck hard, deriving a loud groan from the Adonis. I continue to tease, softly stroking his thighs with my fingernails, this heightens his plea for entry. He is sitting on the edge of the bed with me straddling his waist and he can no longer take the denial. He stands up and forces himself into me resulting in a shriek of delight from both of us. We can feel how wet and warm the entry is, I lie backwards down the length of the Adonis's legs with his member firmly engulfed inside of me. Upside down I look up to the Adonis as he thrusts and thrusts with all his might while holding my arms and my full body weight in his upright stance. The sweat pours from him profusely, he tries to keep me from falling even though our bodies are slick with sweat and our grip is loosening. I hold onto his strong forearms whilst he holds tightly onto my thighs, still pounding hard into me. We both feel that we are losing our grip not only on the outside of our bodies but also on the inside. The waves of passion intensify, the convulsions and writhing of our bodies commence in unison until together we explode in passion. Gasping and groaning our hearts pounding. We are spent and fall in a heap, our sweat soaked bodies clinging to each other.

Cleansing

With our spent bodies we stagger to the shower as though punch drunk with love, but also longing to be clean and refreshed for our next reunion. The shower is turned on, producing a hot strong force of water pounding down onto our bodies. I pick up the soap, lathering it in my hands then massaging my soapy hands over the Adonis's body. First his chest, then his nipples, which are already erect, but the soft soapy glide only strengthens their resolve in standing to attention. I then move my soapy hands over the Adonis's belly circling around and around, gliding softly over his hips. His member starts to stir. I re-lather my hands and take his member into both soapy hands and glide effortlessly up and down his shaft, making the Adonis moan. His eyes close and his breathing quickens. I thrust a soapy hand under him and between his buttocks, which lubricated by the soap, slide with no effort or friction, then ever so softly into the crack of his bottom. His member, rock solid, stands to its full height beckoning entry. I take a soapy finger and slip it into the Adonis's bottom and he groans with delight. The soap makes entry effortless allowing the full length of my finger to slide into him. He groans again, this time louder. I push my finger backward and forward, there is no friction due to the soap acting as a lubricant easing entry in and out.

The Adonis lathers his hands with soap and massages my breasts in a circular motion. As start to breathe heavier he moves his slippery hands all over my body, eventually reaching my womanhood and pushes two fingers into me, I groan with delight as he tickles my G spot. I can't tell if the ease of entry is due to the soap or my natural juices beckoning him. He turns me around putting my hands on the wall, pulling my hips back and spreading my legs. The anticipation is electrifying. He squats, searching with his member and then thrusts into me, we groan with delight as he slips his full length into me. He thrusts and thrusts, my hands struggle to hold on against the steam on the wall. He holds my hips tight to prevent my movement, anchoring me to the spot so that his thrusts don't falter in attaining maximum depth. I groan with pleasure and his breathing intensifies. I reach down to stimulate my clitoris at the same time he continues to thrust into me. As it is all slippery my fingers glide over my clitoris vigorously, sending sensations deep into my womanhood. I arch my back to enable deeper entry of his manhood. The thrusting speeds up, my clitoris swells as it's stimulated and the Adonis member's head is so hard feeling the clench of my womanhood. I start to convulse and the Adonis feels the intensity urging him to thrust harder and deeper to take me to climax.......we both let out a cry of passion as we explode together. Like death throes the Adonis thrusts spasmodically until he too is spent. He squats to lower his member out of me and embraces me close from behind, we feel the hot water shower over us soothing our heightened nerve endings to

47

a relaxed stance. Our breathing returns to normal and I switch off the shower. Hand-in-hand, we return to bed to sleep holding one another as we know, tomorrow we have to part......

2.7 TIME'S UP

I awaken slowly with a sense of being watched, the Adonis is staring at me, as though his piercing blue eyes are willing me to wake. I smile at him and he smiles back adoringly. I know he has strong feelings for me too. He takes my face tenderly into both his hands and kisses me softly. This is the day I must return him to the market with the fear that I will never see him again. I feel a tear trickle down my cheek and the Adonis kisses it stroking my hair off my forehead saying we will be together, I must just be patient, as he will find a way. I can't help but think it may not happen, how can it be possible? He is not free to be with me; to choose the life he wants. Maybe my time with the Adonis is destined to be short, having our paths crossing on our journey in life. He asks me to trust him that he will do whatever is in his power so that we can be together.

The Adonis starts to caress me, with his hands lightly touching every inch of my body I start to tremble. My nipples become erect, the blood rushes to my breasts so that they are full and inviting. The Adonis flicks my nipples between his thumb and forefinger tightly hurting me, I flinch. He then sucks them hard causing me to squirm uneasily. His hands start to move down my body, I can feel my womanhood tingle with anticipation but as though on purpose to drive me wild, he bypasses and touches me everywhere but there. He turns me over across his knees pouring massage oil over my back, bottom and his hands. He lets it trickle down my bottom and it seeps through finding its way to my womanhood. He massages the oil into my back with firm circling movements, then moves to my bottom making my body very slippery to the touch. His hand then moves between my bottom cheeks, sliding effortlessly to my womanhood, smoothly spreading the oil over my clitoris and entry to my sacred centre but he does not enter, driving me wild. He keeps massaging in a circular motion with his strong hands, kneading my skin, almost to tenderise and make it supple to the touch. It feels so slippery and smooth, I can feel my womanhood beckoning him to enter me but he still hovers on the outskirts. He is teasing, rubbing and caressing whilst my hips start to gyrate in search of his fingers or his manhood, anything to enter me to fulfil my need. He caresses my thighs, his strong oily hands moving effortlessly down my legs until he reaches my foot. He engulfs my big toe with his mouth sucking and licking between my toes, tickling me and sending shivers directly to my core which is aching for entry. He continues to massage up my legs, my legs fall open beckoning him but bypassing, he massages all around to my thighs, hips and stomach, my love juices are flowing, trickling onto his thighs. He pushes me off of his knees letting my legs fall to the ground, with my bottom exposed, my face and torso lying on the bed, he kneels behind me. I can feel my womanhood clenching with the anticipation of his entry. He pins my back down with one hand so I cannot move and plunges his manhood into me. With a gasp of delight from us both he thrusts as fast and deep as he can filling me to capacity with his length. He grasps my hair in one hand pulling my head up slightly to kiss me, the discomfort causes my muscles to tense and tighten all over my body including around his manhood. My clitoris is aching to be touched, to apply some pressure I try to rub against the bed with each thrust. The Adonis can see my needs and flips me over onto my back, legs still spread apart hanging over the bed. He bends down, clutching my thighs with his strong hands, he dives in with his mouth to lick and suck my clitoris which is swollen, aching and sensitive to touch. I

50

squirm with delight and rhythmically thrust into his mouth. He pushes two fingers into me and I can feel the warm juices flow freely, easing his entry. He thrusts vigorously with his fingers whilst flicking my clitoris with his tongue. I can feel the pressure building as my body prepares to climax. My pulsating hips push hard against his mouth and fingers wanting more and more. My body starts to convulse until my womanhood clenches tight jerking and thrusting through the waves of climax. I fall in a heap of exhaustion and the Adonis softly licks my clitoris, this makes my body jump like it's received an electric shock as the nerve endings are over charged. The Adonis scoops up my love juices and smears them on my chest, replenishing until he has enough to rub his manhood between my breasts. He pushes my breasts close together making an artificial tunnel, slippery and soft. As he thrusts, my breasts jiggle either side of his manhood. I lubricate my finger with juice from my womanhood and gently push it into the Adonis's bottom. I then slowly begin to match my finger thrusts with his manhood thrusts. The Adonis groans and thrusts harder and harder while I continue to thrust my finger in and out matching his speed. I can see he is in ecstasy but want to take it the next level. I caress his skin sack softly, jiggling it to match the thrusts of my finger in his bottom and his manhood between my breasts. The Adonis is groaning louder and louder, he convulses, pumping hard and jerking until he is spent.

We fall into each other's embrace and kiss tenderly as though being etched into our minds and our very souls, longing to hold onto this feeling forever.

Today is the day to return the Adonis to the marketplace. Our time together has come to an end. I feel so sad with strong feelings that we are destined to be together, but how? I cannot afford to hire the Adonis again. The auctioneer will ensure that the slave seduction results in varying winners to keep the crowd engaged and excited. We walk towards the marketplace hand in hand, we stop, look at each other and the Adonis takes my face in his hands, kisses me tenderly and says "I love you". A tear trickles down my cheek and I say "I love you too". We release each other and the Adonis walks to the market area where the other slaves have congregated. I cannot stay to watch the next slave seduction ritual as cannot bear anyone else to be with my Adonis. I must walk away even though I feel my heart breaking as I find it hard to be apart from him.

The days that follow leave me full of sadness and feeling empty as though part of me is missing. I cry myself to sleep each night wishing my Adonis was with me entwined with me, body and soul. I suddenly awaken in the middle of the night with loud banging on my front door. My heart is pounding with fright, who could it be at this late hour? I drag on my robe and rush to the door opening it gingerly. There I find the Adonis standing before me. I am shocked, how could this be? I am so happy to see him and embrace him tightly and him me. We kiss passionately feeling our connection stronger than ever. The Adonis explains that the auctioneer has died of a heart attack, therefore his slave contract is null and void and he is now free. Free to be with me! I am so excited I cry with joy, kissing him again. The Adonis picks me up and carries me back into the house to the bedroom and we lie, entwined together forever.

3   EROTIC ENCOUNTERS WITH A DJ

Ron is a local radio DJ. Carol listens to his show each week enjoying the music which brings back fond memories of her childhood. Although she lives alone, Carol leads a hectic life. After a long week she really looks forward to sitting back and relaxing with a stiff drink while tuning in to the radio show. Ron has a great voice, very soothing, comforting and really quite sexy. Carol is mesmerised, feeling a strong connection to Ron even though she isn't with him. A lot of the songs are love songs and as Carol listens intently to the words, she imagines that the songs are romantically directed at her like secret messages to her soul.

Carol relaxes on her sofa, tuned into Ron's show. She pictures him sitting at his desk, poised in front of the microphone in the studio. The music blaring as he works the dials and buttons to sync the next song into play. Her imagination runs wild, thinking of what she would do to him if she were there. Her mind wanders and she drifts into a daydream, picturing their encounter....

In her sleek black sports car, she drives up to the radio station, wearing black sunglasses, a short black dress and no underwear. Carol parks her car towards the back of the carpark, alongside Ron's powerful V8, hoping to be discreet as she walks confidently into the studio. While still wearing her black sunglasses, Carol strides confidently past the receptionist stating that she is here to see Ron, who is expecting her. The receptionist shouts after Carol saying "you can't go in there Ron's on air." Carol knows that but continues on. As she walks through the door she sees that Ron is in his usual attire, jeans, t-shirt and a baseball cap. Ron has the most beautiful smooth, soft, and tanned skin. Carol waits until Ron finishes addressing the audience on the past three songs played and sets off the next trio of tunes. Ron looks surprised to see Carol but is secretly pleased, she looks amazing, as always, and his heart skips a beat.

Carol walks over to Ron and kisses him on the cheek inhaling his Calvin Klein after shave. She leans in close, snuggling into his soft neck while breathing in deeply, she then lets out a contented sigh as this has become her happy place where she finds peace and safety in the arms of Ron. Carol reaches up and softly kisses Ron on the lips, she then glides her tongue over his lips as though applying lipstick. Her tongue enters his mouth and she can feel his warm breath as he responds to her kiss. He holds her face in his hands, kissing her softly and gently whilst caressing her face with his thumb. He moves his thumb across her cheek bone as though wiping away invisible tears in a gesture of protective love.

They were alerted to the clip clop of high heels in the corridor, as the receptionist walks up to Ron's studio. Carol quickly ducks down under the desk, Ron sits down and pulls his chair closer to the turntable and microphone. The receptionist walks in and apologises to Ron for the interruption by the woman who forced her way into the studio and looks around trying to find her. Ron says "what woman?" The receptionist looks puzzled thinking the woman must have gone to another studio or the toilets, she turns around exiting Ron's studio to continue her search. Ron whispers down to Carol "you're not supposed to be in here whilst I'm on air" and Carol replies "don't worry, pretend I'm not here". Ron clicks the microphone on as the set concludes and outlines the songs and artists he just played for his audience. Meanwhile, Carol starts to slowly unzip Ron's jeans, then drags her fingernails over his denim thighs pulling his jeans down, he wriggles to help her succeed. She pulls the jeans down to his ankles anchoring him there so he cannot escape. On her hands and knees she slowly blows her warm breath up his thighs and the hair on his legs tickle with the movement. Ron feels Carol pull his black Calvin Klein briefs over his hips, he lifts up to enable them to be pulled down his legs to his ankles. Ron can feel the cool air all over the bottom half of his exposed body and feels an excitement which is apparent from his throbbing member pointing up to the underside of his desk. Tender kisses are then planted over Ron's soft warm furry belly and Carol flicks her tongue into his belly button. Holding Ron's thighs in place Carol blows warm breath over the hair on his testicles sending tingles through his groin, she sees his member respond, it flicks, searching for the source of pleasure.

Ron continues to host his show but falters when he goes to air. His voice quivering as he is being pleasured under the desk unbeknownst to his listeners. Carol runs her fingernails softly down his thighs followed by soft kisses. As she softly licks the length of his shaft she allows saliva to escape, lubricating his member so that her mouth can engulf him fully and glide with ease. She flicks the tip of his member with her tongue, this makes Ron groan with pleasure. She pushes his legs apart so she can gain deeper access into his groin. She inhales his scent as she pushes her face into his scrotum holding the top of his thighs, breathing him in, taking his skin between her teeth and softly tugging, making him squirm. She grabs his hips with both hands and pulls him closer, his member goes deep into her mouth and Ron lets out of cry of pleasure.

There is a voice from the door, the receptionist pops her head in and asks Ron if he had called out to her. Ron quickly replies no, and adds that he was just singing along to the music. Carol is well hidden and the receptionist is not aware that Ron is being pleasured, whilst sitting behind his desk, with his pants around his ankles. Carol smirks as she revels in the situation of them taking a huge risk. The thought of being caught certainly heightens her own excitement and she can feel herself becoming extremely wet. Her short black dress with no underwear conceals the love juice trickling down her inner thighs.

Carol continues to suck Ron's member, softly at first and then she quickens the pace, gently massaging his shaft and testicles with her hands while sucking tighter and tighter. Ron fully relaxes, sliding down the seat and hanging over, this gives Carol the prime opportunity to lubricate her middle finger with her own juices and slide it gently into Ron's bottom. Pushing deeper and deeper allows Ron to feel the full force of the pressure of the sucking of his member as well as the deep penetration into his body, this heightens his pleasure. Ron holds the desk with both hands, he feels so aroused, almost struggling to maintain composure. Ron desperately wants to be inside Carol who sensing this, turns on all fours whilst remaining under the desk. She pulls her black dress up to her hips and exposes her naked smooth rounded bottom which is like porcelain. She starts to arch her back and her glistening inner thighs seem to beckon him to enter her. Ron grabs Carol's hips and thrusts his tongue deep into her, licking her warm soft skin and sucking up her juices. He then flicks her clit with his tongue sucking it hard which drives Carol wild with wanting him inside her. Ron continues to lick her juicy lips, he sucks them, slurping up the dribbles that escape down her thighs. Ron can see that Carol can't wait any longer, he pushes two fingers into her rubbing her G spot with significant pressure. This makes Carol feel the sensation that she is about to explode shouting out "OMG" as her senses go on overload. Ron knows Carol is close to climax so grabs her hips and plunges his member into her. He tries to slow it down to savour the love making for longer, pulling out slowly to the tip then pushing back in very slowly, pulling out slowly to the tip then pushing back in slowly to full capacity. Ron does this a few more times but Carol can't hold on any longer and shouts "GO, GO, GO, faster, harder." Ron thrusts vigorously, increasing the speed and intensity. Carol starts to massage her clit which makes her tighten around Ron's member. They can feel how wet Carol is as Ron glides with ease, love juice trickles down their legs as though they are merging as one. Ron starts to thrust faster and faster, Carol pulsates, pushing back onto him to drive him deeper into her. Ron's grip on Carol's hips tighten as he can feel the crescendo of climax rising, he pulls her hips backwards, ramming his member fast and with full force causing Carol to cry out with pleasure. Their bodies convulse and they let out a deep groan of passion, panting breathlessly while continuing to thrust spasmodically like they are in the death throes. They collapse in a heap under the desk and hold each other tight, not wanting to let go. Ron is spooning Carol, holding her tightly, he ensures that the length of his body is tucked in snugly with Carol's. Carol takes his hand and holds it on her heart, so that he can feel her strong heart beat which beats for him. They are locked together as one and their love for each other permeates every cell of their bodies.

At that moment Carol snaps out of her daydream…. finding herself in her home, in the foetal position on her sofa. The radio show was still playing and Ron on air exclaiming that he hoped everyone had enjoyed the show tonight and to tune in next week. Carol can feel that she is soaking wet from her fantasy. Sighing she thinks that she can't wait until the next show to dream of her erotic encounters with Ron, her new love, the local DJ!

4 EROTIC ENCOUNTERS WITH A BARMAN

Leonie, a long leggy blonde wearing a white dress that hugged her slender figure, walked into the bar. Her eyes were stunning and she had an amazing smile. She walked up to the bar and Dave the Barman asked "What would you like?" She smirked replying "What are you offering?" Dave responded "You can have anything you like", with a glint in his eye admiring her playfulness. She looked into his big blue eyes and adoringly admired his strong muscular body which stood six feet tall. She said "How about you?" Dave was very attracted to Leonie and replied "I finish in ten minutes" She said "I hope not ... but I'll wait for you to finish work" giggling. After composing herself she asked for a Bacardi and Coke no ice in a short glass. She then proceeded to sit directly across the room at a tall table with stools. She put her bag on the floor, bending right over accentuating her long legs and tight ass. Dave couldn't concentrate whilst the next customer ordered as he couldn't stop looking at her curvy body and fantasising what he would be doing to it later.

He quickly filled the order and started clearing up the bar, he was on a mission to get out of there. Leonie sat on the stool, legs crossed looking right over at him watching his every move. She sucked on the straw provocatively, making his groin tingle as he thought of how she would be sucking his straw later. She pulled out her lipstick and reapplied then blew him a kiss. Dave was ready to finish work and handed over to Simon, the other Barman, who took over. Dave walked over to Leonie and said "Are you ready for the ride of your life?" She said "Always." She stood up and took his hand, he led her to his sports car parked outside. He took the roof off and drove towards the countryside. He watched the wind blowing her hair which made her look like the wild woman, he hoped she was. He turned down a lonely lane, there were no street lights, no people, no houses and no cars!

He pulled over. Leonie started to get worried she may have put herself in danger. Dave could sense her fear and said "Don't worry. I want to make love to you not hurt you." He went around and opened her car door. She stepped out. He took her hand and proceeded to the front of the car. She thought they were going to go somewhere but he stopped at the front of the car, the headlights were on. He started to touch her softly, kissing her gently and holding her face in his hands. She melted, feeling safe and secure in his gentle touch. He lifted her dress over her head and she stood in white lacy underwear. She had a beautiful body, perfect breasts, rounded hips and she stood only in white high heels, lacy white underwear, silhouetted by the shining headlights of the car. He started to caress her, touching her softly, gliding his hands over her toned body and pulling her closer to him. She held his face and kissed him passionately, moving her hands down to his shirt she undid the buttons one by one. Opening his shirt revealed a muscular chest and shoulders and a soft belly. She slipped his shirt off and let her fingers glide down his chest and flick over his nipples. Leaning over she licked his nipples, circling her tongue around the erect pimple as it grew harder and harder. Her hands moved to his belt and undid it, followed by unzipping his fly and pushing his jeans down over his hips.

He stood there in tight black Calvin Klein underwear which clung to his body, his protruding member swelling in anticipation. She pulled the briefs down to his ankles and his manhood sprang out, standing to attention. She touched it softly gliding her hand up and down the shaft, feeling its warmth and hardness. Kneeling down she started to kiss it softly, all the way along the shaft and up onto the tip. Cupping his balls in her one hand, she massaged them slowly feeling him growing bigger in her other hand. She licked the head of his member, circling around the tip and then licking inside the slit at the top of his shaft. Dribbling saliva over the tip then engulfing his member into her mouth, she slowly took it all in gliding slowly over the length of his shaft. He groaned with pleasure as she slowly and sensually sucked. He reached to pull her undies down so that he could explore her. He put his hand underneath her and feeling that her juices had started to flow, moist, warm and soft. He moved his hands to her breasts and undid her bra, releasing her plentiful breasts to the cold air. Her nipples were erect; he didn't know if it was because she was cold or because she was excited but decided it was a combination of both. He cupped her breasts in his hands, lifted one up to his mouth and starting to suck her erect nipple. She groaned with pleasure and her breathing started to increase in pace. He sucked hard making her wince.

He then laid her back on the bonnet which was still warm from the drive. Completely naked she lay on the bonnet, he lifted her legs up onto his shoulders, pulling her close to him so her bottom was on the edge where the lights were bright. He could see her love juices glistening in the light and it stirred his member which was anxiously awaiting entry into this beautiful creature. He hugged her thighs to him and pushed his full length into her. She let out a cry of pleasure and gripped his forearms tightly. He held her legs so that she couldn't move and thrust his member deep inside her. The car rocked a bit with the force and she splayed her arms across the bonnet to gain balance. His thrust was slow and deep, he was savouring the moment and enjoying feeling her warm soft moistness around his member. He pulled out, stood her up and turned her around. Requesting that she bend over, put her hands on the bonnet with her feet apart. She obeyed standing there in her high heels, her long legs bent with her bare bottom arched back beckoning him to re-enter. He started to kiss the back of her thighs softly and she was trembling.

He tapped her legs indicating that he wanted her to spread them more to which she complied. He pushed her down onto the bonnet, bending her right over with her forearms resting on the car and her belly on the edge. The car lights shone right through the gap between her outstretched legs, he could see the shining love juices that had trickled down her inner thighs. He squatted behind her using his tongue to lick up her thighs and collect her juices as she continued to tremble and groan with delight. He held her legs still and licked her swollen wet lips. They were so wet and warm and her clitoris was swollen waiting to be touched. He sucked her clit, pulling it like a teat, sucking backwards and forwards while extending it to heighten her pleasure. Leonie was in ecstasy, groaning loudly she pushed her bottom backwards to guide his mouth into her. She couldn't stand waiting for him to re-enter her, she was longing for his member to be inside her, filling her, stretching her. Dave stood up and took Leonie's hips and plunged his engorged manhood deep into her and thrust vigorously. She reached down to massage her clit, he was thrusting in and out of her with force pushing her further onto the car. The pace increased and they were both groaning with pleasure, she was thrusting back onto him and he matched her pace pushing deep into her. The pressure grew and grew until both their bodies started to jerk in spasms, they came together, crying out loudly, sending an echo across the silent countryside. Dave thrust jerkily a few more times as though he was emptying his last drops into her. He slumped onto her back with his arms laid along hers entwining their fingers. Their heartbeats were racing; their breath was laboured as they were both spent.

5 EROTIC ENCOUNTERS AT A WAREHOUSE

Carl has a small warehouse where he stores his classic cars. He goes to the warehouse weekly to check on the cars, give them a polish as he feels great pride in his collection. He daydreams about taking the classic cars out for a drive with a beautiful woman in the passenger seat to share the experience.

One day, Carl was at the warehouse, ensuring they were all covered to allow no dust to get onto their shiny bodies. A woman calls out from the front roller door saying that she has a parcel to deliver. Carl walks up to the front of the warehouse wondering what the parcel could be as he hadn't ordered anything. He suddenly stops in his tracks, standing before him is a long legged brunette, large blue eyes, dressed in a maid's outfit. He looked a bit shocked, she asked "Is your name Carl?" He stammers "yes" and she says "great, I have been sent as your parcel for you to do with me whatever you desire."

Carl can't believe it and thinks it's possibly a joke, but she moves closer to him, he sees she has bountiful breasts which are pushing up out of her white frilly top. Her black skirt is so small it shows off her very long slender legs. She does a twirl which causes her skirt to puff out displaying her black G-string. This shows off her taut bottom which looks silky soft. She takes his hand and walks him down the back of the warehouse where they can't be seen. She starts to unbutton his shirt; his nipples are erect with anticipation. She flicks his nipples with her tongue leaving saliva over them so that her tongue glides effortlessly in circles around them. She undoes his shirt and uses it to tie his wrists behind his back, she has pushed him up against one of his classic cars. His tanned body is taut, his nipples erect and she starts to unzip his jeans feeling his member pushing hard up against the zipper, waiting to pounce into action like a jack-in-the-box.

She pulls his jeans down over his thighs and to the ground, she then slips his underwear off too. He is stood naked with his hands tied behind his back and a huge erection. He is so excited but scared that someone may come into the warehouse and catch them. He can hear cars outside and passers by walking to other warehouse units. The "maid" bends down and runs her fingernails up his thighs, his member is moving about frantically as though anticipating her touch, but she makes him wait. She starts to unbutton her frilly white blouse letting her milky white breasts fall out with her pink nipples erect. She bends down and pushes her breasts together to make a tight tunnel, dribbling saliva

69

to lubricate it, she puts Carl's stiff rod up into her breast tunnel. It is very tight but slippery wet from her saliva. She starts to push up and down taking Carl's member on a ride, pushed in tight between her breasts. Carl feels the skin on his member burning with the friction being created, but loves the sensation.

The maid then stands up, she unzips her skirt letting it drop to the ground, revealing her black G-string. Standing before him is this slender woman wearing only a G-string, her breasts engorged awaiting to be sucked. She unties Carl's wrists, he anxiously cups her breasts into his hands, licking and sucking her nipples hungrily. Her breasts are soft and supple and her nipples rock hard. She moans with pleasure and takes his manhood into her hand, she starts to glide her hand up and down along the shaft gently massaging it. Carl wants to last a long time and says "wait" …. He walks over to fetch the car jack. It is a large one with quite a substantial plate, it can be jacked up to six feet tall to allow for cars to be lifted and worked on from underneath. Carl starts to jack it up to waist height asking the maid to sit on it and lie back with her arms above her head for balance. The maid lies across the jack while Carl starts to pump it higher until it is nearly six feet tall and right in front of his face, there he positions the maid's honeypot. He takes her legs, resting her feet on his shoulders and asks if she is comfortable. Once she confirms, he starts to softly lick her swollen lips which are now very moist and warm. She groans with pleasure as he sucks her clit and puts his fingers deep into her, releasing her juices which flow down onto his hand. He slurps hungrily with his mouth sucking up her juices and pushing his tongue into her, she feels so soft and his tongue glides in and out effortlessly. The maid is in ecstasy and she grabs his head to pull him in deeper. Carl uses his two fingers to push inside her and rubs her G spot slowly, then starts to increase the pace. She is groaning louder, exclaiming that she wants him inside her, but he tells her to wait. He kisses along her thighs and then takes one of her feet, puts her big toe into his mouth and sucks it…it really tickles and she squirms. He can tell she likes it as her juices continue to flow, glistening around her love lips.

He decides it's time to let her down and tells her to hold on whilst he releases the jack. He takes her by the hand, walking her over to one of the classic cars and opening the back door. He slides in and sits in the middle of the back seat with his legs behind each of the front seats. His member is still standing to attention and he wants her on top of him really bad. He asks her to get into the car and straddle him. She climbs over and he helps her straddle his lap, she lowers herself down onto his manhood and as he pushes it in slowly she cries out in pleasure and starts to ride him. As she moves up and down and her breasts jiggle before his eyes, he grabs them, sucking hard and pushing himself deep into her.

Continuing to ride up and down she changes position, turning around to ride him facing out the windscreen, holding his legs riding him up and down with him under her. Carl doesn't want to cum, he pushes her forward so that she is lying between the two front seats. He pulls out and moves her so that she is on all fours, this allows him to lick her again whilst stimulating her G spot with his fingers. This is driving her wild, she pushes back on him, groaning with pleasure. He decides to change position again, moving out of the car he tells her to lie along the back seat and bring her bottom to the edge at the car door. He lifts her legs straight up against his body, her feet on either side of his head with that he holds tightly onto her thighs and plunges his member into her pumping hard and deep. They are both crying out with pleasure as the pace intensifies, they can feel the pressure building until their bodies convulse and they spasmodically thrust into one another yelling out as though in excruciating pain, but it is ultimate ecstasy. Sweat is dripping down Carl's chest as he pumps hard and fast. Panting and holding each other tight they jerk through their last convulsion. Carl is slumped on top of the "maid", their slippery bodies sticking together and they wished they could stay like this forever.

Once they had caught their breath Carl helps her out of the car, thanking her profusely for the wonderful surprise. He asks who sent her and she said "no one". It turns out she had seen him around and asked other warehouse owners what his name was as she knew she just had to have him. They exchanged numbers and agreed to rendezvous again very soon. He promised her that they would go for a drive to the ocean in one of his classic cars. She said she would like that and kissed him goodbye.

6 EROTIC ENCOUNTERS IN THE BATHTUB

It was the end of the week and Mary wanted to make it a special and romantic evening for when John got home from work. They had moved into their new home, which they had designed themselves, a few months ago. They loved their dream home, Mary contributed a lot of input into the bathroom design, because she loved spa baths and wanted a sensual and relaxing space for them to unwind, connect and enjoy each other's bodies.

Mary got to work, making the bathroom a haven of romance by decorating it with many lit candles. She sprinkled rose petals over the vanity and edges of the huge square spa bath. The bath was in front of a large picture window which overlooked the ocean, providing privacy, as they were elevated up the side of a cliff.

The large fluffy white bath towels were hung on the warming towel rack, a bottle of chilled champagne & glasses sat on the wide ledge alongside the bath with a large platter of cheeses, meats, strawberries, chocolate dipping sauce and crackers.

John was due home in 10 minutes, Mary hurried to get the romantic soft music set up and put on her satin robe with nothing on underneath. She heard the car pull up on the drive and she rushed into the bathroom, put the plug in, added bubble bath and turned on the taps to start filling their love pool. Mary was so excited and greeted John at the door, He had a bunch of yellow roses for her, her favourite colour, a wonderful surprise. John handed the flowers to Mary and grabbed her in his arms giving her a big kiss. Mary responded passionately and was glad that John was feeling romantic too. She knew he would love the little love haven she had set up for them. Mary took John's hand and led him to the bathroom, and with a big smile on his face he exclaimed "What's all this then". He loved it when Mary was spontaneous, she certainly kept their love life exciting.

Mary helped John peel off his shirt, whilst he was undoing his belt and unzipping his pants she was running her fingertips down his torso, sucking at his nipples flicking them with her tongue. John's nipples stood erect with excitement and when he pulled his pants down to the floor she could see his member spring to life, pleading for some attention. The bath was still running so Mary took John's hand and led him into their double shower, it was huge giving them plenty of room to play. Mary slipped off her gown and stepped into the shower with John, his back to her. Mary picked up the soap, lathered some in her hands and started to massage the suds into Johns back, pressing firmly to ease away the stress of the day. She let the suds float down his back and slither between his butt cheeks.

Mary lathered up some more and took her hand underneath John between his legs, he spread his legs to give her access. With soft suds on her hand she massaged his balls and took her fingers back up through his butt cheeks, gliding softly. She went back under again, all the way to the front feeling his member standing at attention. Mary turned John around, when he was facing her with water trickling down his face and his torso, she admired what a handsome man he was and she felt so in love with him. Mary lathered up again and took John's member in her hand, gliding it up and down with ease from the sudsy lubricant.

John lathered up his hands and ran his palms over Mary's breasts feeling the hard nipples that were already erect with the excitement of their play. John turned Mary around and pushed her against the wall, her hands slapped against the tiles to gain some grip. She parted her legs bending over, anticipating John's entry but to her surprise John was on his knees, he licked her love lips which made Mary groan with pleasure. She bent over to give him more access, he held her hips and continued to lick her slurping at her love juices which started to flow. He stood up, knees bent and using his hand he guided his manhood into Mary who cried out with pleasure as she grasped at the bathroom wall. Mary pushed back towards John, bending over more so he could get in deeper. John thrust into Mary holding her hips still as he drove his member deep into her. Mary was moaning and groaning, she loved John making love to her from behind, it was her favourite position. John grabbed Mary's shoulders with both hands thrusting a few more times before stopping and pulling out so that he could last.

John noticed that the bath was ¾ full, he stepped out of the shower to turn off the taps. Mary turned the shower off following John to the bathtub, she got in sitting between his legs lying up against his chest. They both sighed and John said "how about we have some champagne". Mary agreed and sat up so John could do the honours. John poured the champagne into the two glasses handing one to Mary. They clinked glasses, saying "I love you" on cue and sipped.

Mary offered the platter to John who took some delights to munch on whilst he sipped his champagne. Mary asked John to sit up on the wide ledge at the end of the bath to continue his champagne. She parted his legs and told him to move his bottom closer to the edge. Mary dipped a strawberry into the chocolate and lightly slid it along John's shaft, circling the tip and letting the chocolate coat it. She then popped the strawberry into John's mouth whilst she licked the chocolate that had dribbled down John's shaft.

She ran her tongue the full length, swirling the chocolate at the very tip of the head and flicked it with her tongue. John stroked Mary's hair lovingly and smiled as she took his member into her mouth, she started to suck it while working the shaft with her hand. John groaned and Mary caressed his balls with her other hand. She pushed John back so he was lying down and she grabbed some bath suds to lubricate her hand, her finger searched for entry into his bottom. She pushed her finger slowly in and out to match the rhythm with her sucking and thrusting of his shaft. John was in ecstasy loving every moment. After a while John said "let me do you now" so Mary switched places with him. She lay on the ledge, her feet up on the edge and her bottom hanging over to give John access. John held onto Mary's thighs and started licking her up and down her love lips then sucking her clitoris which drove Mary wild. He dipped his finger into the chocolate and put it inside Mary, he then ate hungrily pushing his tongue in deeper to extract the chocolate. John dipped his finger into the chocolate again and smothered it on Mary's clit, he then licked and flicked his tongue sucking up the chocolate until it was all gone.

John pushed his finger inside Mary and curled it up behind to apply pressure on her G spot, she groaned with pleasure. John put two fingers in and out vigorously then slowing to apply pressure on the G spot again. Mary was crying out with pleasure and John knew she wanted him inside her. John said "Let me sit there and you sit on my lap", so Mary stepped up to allow John to sit down and she sat backwards easing herself up and down onto his member going faster and faster. John held her hips so she wouldn't lose her balance before suggesting they get out of the bath. Mary stepped out and John pulled the towels off the warming rack drying Mary then himself. He then turned Mary around to face the towel rack and pushed her onto it, she flinched as her nipples felt the heat. John held her there then used the towels to tie Mary's hands to it. He pulled her hips towards him to force her to bend over and pushed her legs apart. He started to kiss Mary's inner thighs softly, then parting her butt cheeks, with tiny flicks of his tongue he pushed against Mary's bottom circling the entry which was so sensitive and drove Mary wild. Her love juices really started to flow and John allowed his tongue to glide under her to slurp up the juices and suck her love lips into his mouth.

John stood up and ran his hands softly down Mary's back then around to caress her bountiful breasts. He squeezed her nipples between his thumbs and forefingers massaging them as they grew harder and harder. Mary grasped the warm towel rack feeling the heat in her hands but it wasn't as hot as she felt between her legs. She could feel herself tingling with anticipation, she was so hot for John to be inside her. John could sense her anticipation and asked her "do you want me" and she exclaimed "yes". He said "but do you really want me" and she said "yes I really do, please make love to me."

John walked around behind Mary and slapped her on the bottom making her squeal, he then ran his fingernails of both hands up each butt cheek leaving red marks. Mary pushed back towards John beckoning him to enter. He put his hand under her and felt how wet she was, then ran his fingernails of both hands down the full length of her back, which she arched, grimacing. There were long red welts down her back and buttocks. John tapped her inner thigh as a signal to widen her legs apart, Mary obliged as she couldn't wait much longer. She pleaded, "John, make love to me". John decided he wanted Mary secured in one position so he could take her without her being able to move. John grabbed another towel and lifted Mary's left leg up and tied her foot to the towel rack. Mary couldn't move. John loved having Mary in this vulnerable position. As he stuck his fingers into her, her love juices flowed with anticipation, oozing through his fingers. He pushed them in and out and Mary was groaning with pleasure. While John was rubbing her clitoris he knew she wasn't far from climaxing as Mary was crying out loudly with pleasure. The vulnerable position she was in, with John dominating her, made her feel so erotic that she couldn't wait much longer.

John stood in close behind her, held her left thigh which was elevated, and plunged his manhood deep into Mary who shrieked with pleasure. John thrust hard and fast into Mary who was so wet and warm that he glided with ease. He reached around and pinched a nipple between his fingers, this made Mary flinch with pain and contract around his member. John then reached around rubbing Mary's clit whilst he continued to thrust deep and fast with Mary clinging onto the towel rack so tight, moaning loudly with pleasure. Mary started to tighten and groan deeply, John knew she was about to cum. He quickened his pace and pushed deep into Mary as hard as he could, he started to jerk spasmodically, yelling out with pleasure while oozing his last drops into Mary. She too was convulsing in climax. They both were panting heavily and John slumped onto

Mary's back kissing her shoulder, saying "I love you". Mary said "I love you more" and they giggled.

John untied Mary and they both hopped into the bath. Mary sat between John's legs lying back on his chest. They both sighed and he wrapped his arms around her to pull her close to him. They then soaked in the bath, drank champagne and ate the nibbles as they had certainly worked up a hunger.

7   EROTIC ENCOUNTERS ON THE BEACH

The ambience of the restaurant, dimly lit, with swaying palm trees and overlooking the ocean made for a romantic setting for Tony and Monica. It was a special night, their anniversary, and it had been awhile since they had time alone without their kids. Tony thought Monica looked absolutely radiant, her eyes sparkled and she looked beautiful. He thought how busy their life was with their everyday routine, and realised that he hadn't stopped every once in a while to truly just sit and admire his stunning wife.

After a lovely dinner Tony and Monica were driving home via the coastal road and as it was a balmy night they had the roof off. Tony thought Monica looked exceptionally beautiful as the moonlight illuminated her face and the wind blew her hair. Monica could sense Tony looking at her, she turned and smiled at him, reaching across to hold his hand as he drove. It was so nice for the two of them to be alone, like the old days out on a date, this made them both feel very romantic.

Tony took a turn off towards the beach and suggested a romantic walk. He parked close to the sand dunes. Monica said "what a lovely idea" and flipped off her sandals leaving her floating dress to wrap around her legs clinging to her curvy body as the wind blew. They walked down the beach path hand in hand.

As they walked along the beach Tony said "you look very lovely tonight" and stopped to give Monica a passionate kiss. He held her face in his hands, kissing her softly and tenderly before leading her into the sand dunes. There was no one around, the cool breeze off the ocean made them feel alive and eager to make love amongst nature under the stars.

Tony lifted Monica's dress off over her head, admiring her beautiful body, curvy hips, milky white porcelain skin and perky breasts. She was wearing lacy underwear which made her look so sexy and feminine that he couldn't keep his hands off her. He undid her bra to release her breasts into the cool breeze, this instantly aroused her nipples which stood to attention beckoning his touch. Tony cupped one of her breasts in his hand and licked around the nipple before sucking it gently. His other hand reached down into her panties, he felt her arousal as her love lips were moist and warm, awaiting his touch. He took her panties off and she stood vulnerable and naked to the elements of nature.

Monica started to unbutton Tony's shirt and slipped it off of his shoulders. He had a toned body which was muscular and

84

tanned. Monica then kissed his chest softly with little kisses as she made her way up to his lips and kissed him sensually. She then unzipped his trousers where his member was waiting for some attention. She pulled his trousers and underpants down to the sand and removed them from his ankles. They both stood naked. She stayed down at his mid-level and pushed his legs apart giving her access to his undercarriage.

She could see that he was very aroused, the cool breeze was blowing the hair on his genitals which made him sensitive to touch. She took his erect member in her hand and slowly blew her warm breath onto it, up and down the shaft. She licked the length and circled the head with her tongue, dribbling saliva over it. She then took his member fully into her mouth and slowly sucked it up and down whilst caressing his balls with her other hand. She felt underneath him and dribbled saliva onto her fingers before caressing him under his scrotum finding entry into him where she slipped a finger deep into his cavity. Taken by surprise, he gasped and grabbed her shoulders. The sensation was always intrusive but so erotic. She moved her finger inside him and sucked up and down his shaft in perfect rhythm. He was groaning with pleasure, holding himself steady with his hands on her shoulders. He then pulled her up to him and suggested she sit on him as he lay on the sand.

He lay down, she was soaking wet with love juice trickling down her thighs as she wanted him inside her so badly. She straddled him, letting his member slowly slide its full length into her. She groaned with pleasure as he pushed himself deep into her and she started to ride him up and down as he thrust up into her, both in sync, riding each other like riding the waves they could hear crashing nearby.

Monica kissed Tony passionately whilst he still thrust into her, grabbing her breasts that were dancing freely in time to their thrusts and he hungrily sucked a hard nipple. This made Monica groan, Tony could feel her contract around his member as the excitement grew. He started thrusting faster and she sat upright riding him up and down with her breasts bouncing to the rhythm. He licked his thumb and used it to rub Monica's clitoris which drove her wild with passion. He was rubbing it faster and faster whilst pumping her hard.

They wanted to savour the love making and not cum too soon so they changed position. She went on all fours over him, her face in line with his member and his with her honeypot, and slowly they explored each other's sacred place with their mouths. Monica dribbled saliva onto Tony's member and sucked it whilst holding his thighs. Tony had Monica's honeypot above his mouth, he pulled her down so he could lick up her juices that were flowing freely and flicking her clit with his tongue before sucking it, sending shivers up Monica's spine. She arched her back and pushed down into his face. Tony pushed his fingers into Monica feeling the love juices ooze as he pulled them out then pushed them back again. Monica was groaning with pleasure which reverberated along Tony's shaft as it was being sucked up and down tighter and tighter. The more pleasure Monica felt the harder she sucked.

Monica sucked her finger and slipped it slowly into Tony's bottom making him groan with pleasure. She moved her finger in and out whilst massaging his balls with her other hand and sucking his member. So many sensations were driving Tony wild. He started to thrust into Monica's mouth pushing deep as his excitement was hard to contain.

Monica stopped delivering pleasure to Tony to extend the moment of climax. She got up and straddled him again but didn't let him inside. She leaned forward over him and dangled her breasts in his face so that he could caress her and play with her nipples. Tony rubbed his palms softly over Monica's nipples, hardly touching them which drove her wild. Monica arched her back and her engorged breasts longed for his touch. He cupped her breast in his hand and took the nipple to his mouth, flicking it with his tongue. Using his other hand, he pinched her other nipple making her flinch.

Monica moved back down Tony's legs and pushed his knees up so she could gain access. Taking Tony's balls in her mouth she sucked them, massaging them with her mouth before pulling back leaving just the skin of the sack that she tugged with her teeth pulling till it could go no more, then sucking it back into her mouth. Tony was groaning with pleasure and his member was rock hard standing tall awaiting some attention.

They were both finding it hard to hold on when Monica moved onto the sand on all fours and Tony got behind her, plunging himself deeply into her he pumped away holding her hips tight. Monica was rubbing her clitoris which was making her tighten around Tony's member, he could feel the pressure around his member been constricted which heightened his arousal. He pumped Monica hard going faster and faster as she pushed back on him to send him deeper.

All of a sudden they let out a huge groan, their bodies convulsed as they both reached ecstasy together thrusting spasmodically as they climaxed. They slumped in a heap, entwined, holding each other as they panted breathlessly, totally spent.

They both slumped into the sand. Lying on their backs, looking up at the stars, that were so bright that night, they held hands and confessed their undying love for each other. Monica said "Let's not wait until our next anniversary until we have spontaneous passion again, let's do this more often". Tony agreed. They got dressed and walked back to the car, hand in hand with big smiles on their faces.

8 EROTIC ENCOUNTERS AT THE CABIN

They were winding down the mountain roads in a black convertible, heading to the cabin they had booked for a weekend away in the Hunter Valley wine region. This weekend getaway is just what Kim and Dave needed to unwind and reconnect. Kim's long brown hair was flowing in the breeze as she looked across at Dave. She thought how handsome he was, tall, blonde with chiselled features and striking blue eyes. Dave looked across and smiled at Kim adoringly, she was his soulmate and he thought it had been too long since they had spent time together, just the two of them. Life had consumed them and they needed to escape their hectic lives for a while.

They turned down the long dirt driveway, made their way up to the cabins and checked in at reception. Kim opened their cabin door and was so impressed with the spacious layout. An open fire in the lounge area was already ablaze making the cabin feel warm and homely. The bedroom, which had a huge king size bed, adorned with many colourful cushions, had sliding glass doors that opened onto a private courtyard backing onto the bush reserve. In the courtyard was a large Jacuzzi that was bubbling away enticing them to soak and relax in the open air.

Dave was carrying the cases and Kim excitedly ran to him saying "you must come and see this" taking him by the hand to show him the Jacuzzi. Dave said "Wow, let's grab a glass of wine and dive in". Dave poured two glasses of wine, they undressed and grabbed the complimentary robes hanging in the wardrobe.

It was so exhilarating to walk outside naked, first into the cold air and then to climb into the Jacuzzi. Lowering themselves into the steamy hot water which bubbled all over their skin. They placed the wine glasses on the ledge and then lay in the water allowing the jets to pound their bodies. The swirling water jiggled Kim's breasts and the bubbles tickled her nipples which were standing erect. Dave could feel the current swirl around his member and balls, swinging them freely with the force of the water. Kim floated over the top of Dave to sit in front of him, he loved seeing Kim's breasts so buoyant, floating yet swaying in the tide of the swishing water. They were glistening wet and looked so smooth like creamy porcelain with dark nipples that were fully erect awaiting Dave's touch. He started to caress Kim's breasts, squeezing her nipples and pulling her closer so that he could take one into his mouth. The bubbles splashed into his face as he hungrily searched for her nipple with his mouth. He latched on and started to suck tenderly whilst continuing to fondle her breasts under the water. He sucked harder extending it to its full stretch. Kim reached under the water and found Dave's rock hard member swaying in the current, she started to massage it up and down allowing her fingernails to glide underneath him stroking his balls. Dave took Kim's face into his hands and kissed her softly. She was such a beautiful woman, with an amazing smile and eyes that penetrated his soul. He then whispered "stand up over the edge of the spa".

Kim stood up and bent over the side of the Jacuzzi exposing her bottom which had water dripping down her soft skin back into the spa. Her breasts hung over the side of the Jacuzzi, engorged, dangling above the ground with water droplets dripping onto the concrete below. Dave let his fingers softly glide down Kim's back, this made her tingle. He kissed Kim's butt cheeks and parted them so he could lick under her and stimulate the flow of her love juices. He started sucking her love lips, extending them as far as they could go then letting them flick back. He flicked his tongue at her clitoris which made Kim groan. She extended her bottom up to Dave enticing him to enter but he made her wait. He knew it was going to be hard to make love in the water as the natural lubricant would be washed away, so he wanted to excite Kim outside the water. He asked her to turn and sit up on the ledge, he then held her thighs over his shoulders, licking her up and down then sucking her clit which made Kim groan. She grabbed his head to guide him and pull him closer. Dave looked up at Kim and could see her breasts glistening wet, her nipples fully erect and hard. He was rock hard himself and wanted to be inside her. He pulled her into the water and quickly straddled her around his waist, thrusting his member into her. Kim cried out as entry was tight and she could feel the friction with each thrust. Dave held her hips tight and thrust up into her, Kim's breasts bounced in and out of the water splashing Dave's face. Kim kissed him passionately, holding the sides of the spa and almost pinning him to the wall of the Jacuzzi, her legs still clung around his waist.

Dave whispered "shall we go inside", and Kim agreed. They got out of the Jacuzzi and wrapped their robes around them. Dave grabbed Kim's hand and led her to the front of the cabin with Kim exclaiming "where are we going?" Dave, being an exhibitionist, revelled in any opportunity of being caught. He pushed Kim up against the trunk of the car, bent her over and moved her robe aside before thrusting into her. Kim groaned putting her hands flat on the trunk to steady herself. Dave thrust deep into her going faster and faster as Kim was moaning with pleasure. Her juices started to flow and Kim had completely forgotten how exposed and vulnerable they were to other patrons staying in nearby cabins. Dave grabbed her hair in his fist and pulled her head up gently exerting his dominance and his other hand in the middle of her back pinning her to the trunk. Dave pumped faster and he could feel her soft, warm moist love canal constrict around his member which drove him wild. Wanting to savour the love making for longer Dave stopped, withdrew and took Kim's hand leading her into the cabin and onto the king sized bed.

Dave took out some toys he had brought from home and placed them on the bed. He got Kim to lie down on her back, naked, whilst he took out his handcuffs and cuffed her hands above her head. He then took up a small whip, which had multiple leather strips and softly glided it up Kim's torso, circling her breasts, gliding it back down her sides which tickled and made Kim squirm. He then moved it down to her thighs, gliding up and down, letting the tassels flick at her soft sensitive skin, then over her love nest bristling her hair. He raised the whip slightly and flicked it, softly whipping Kim's hips, then thighs, then belly, this made Kim flinch but not enough to hurt her. He circled the whip tassels over her nipples which were gaping through the strands, standing erect to the touch.

Dave then switched to a vibrator which had a tickler for the clit and a dildo that vibrated. He gently bent one of Kim's legs so he could gain access and pushed the vibrator inside her which made her groan. He turned the vibrator on, this set Kim off moaning and groaning with pleasure as the vibrations shook her very soul. The tickler vibrated on her clit and the dildo was vibrating against her G spot. Dave moved the vibrator slowly in and out while planting soft kisses on her thighs. The sounds of Kim's pleasure from her groans and her love juices squelching, as the vibrator glided in and out, was driving Dave wild. He decided to switch toys again as he didn't want Kim to cum yet. He pulled the vibrator out and grabbed the big black vibrating wand, one of Kim's favourites. Dave got up to plug it into the power socket. This gave Kim some time for her excitement to wane so that she could be aroused again. Dave took the vibrating wand and placed it on one of Kim's nipples, this stimulated it making Kim breathe heavily. Dave, kneeling next to Kim on the bed, lifted the wand and dribbled saliva down onto the nipple, he then returned the wand to agitate once again. The wand was circling the nipple sending electric waves through her breast. Dave then used the wand down Kim's torso sending vibrations permeating throughout her whole body. Dave took the wand down each thigh and pushed Kim's legs apart again. He then ran the wand over Kim's love lips which made her writhe with pleasure. He could see the glistening wetness start to re-appear and rubbed the wand into the juices, it slid with ease over her clit which drove her crazy. Dave knelt between Kim's splayed legs so he could gain maximum access. With the wand he circled across her love lips and over her clit, more and more juices started to flow. Dave could hear the wand movement squelching, this heightened his arousal.

Kim told Dave to un-cuff her so she could work the magic wand on him. Grabbing the wand, she told Dave to lie down on his back, which he did. Kim took the wand, gliding it up Dave's thighs making his member bounce around with excitement, rock hard anticipating its touch. Kim told Dave to lift his knees up to his stomach, she then moved the wand under Dave, across his butt cheeks, then onto his ball sack which made him groan loudly as it vibrated the loose skin shaking the whole sack around his balls. Kim cupped her hand under his balls to keep them still, she then put the vibrating wand directly onto them which drove Dave wild. He was shouting "oh yeah baby" and his member was waiting patiently for some action. Kim moved the wand up the shaft, this sent vibrations the full length but when it reached the head and started encircling the rim Dave was crying out and thrusting into the wand. Kim, knowing Dave wasn't going to last much longer, took the wand up to his nipple and circled each one as they stood erect. She dribbled saliva onto both so that the wand could glide around the slippery nipples with ease. She then straddled Dave and put the wand to her own nipples which not only excited her, Dave loved to see her nipples respond to the vibration, hear her laboured breath and see the pleasure on her face as her eyes sleepily closed enjoying the moment. Dave reached down to rub Kim's clit which made her groan, she started to rub her love lips, which were oozing love juice, on his thigh.

Kim repositioned herself, straddling Dave in the reverse cowgirl position, lowering herself onto him facing his feet. She sat down hard onto him to take him fully and when Dave pushed into her they both groaned. Kim slowly rose up and down feeling his full length inside her. She rose her body above him, gliding to his tip before slamming down hard, sending him deep into her. She then grabbed the wand, rubbing it on Dave's balls whilst he was thrusting into her as she stayed on top pinning him to the bed. He was groaning as he could feel the vibrations permeate up his shaft whilst he was inside Kim. The warm, soft, wet vibrating love tunnel was driving Dave crazy and he started to thrust faster, Kim knew he was getting close to climax.

She moved the wand onto her clit and started to ride Dave's member whilst he was thrusting deeper and deeper as Kim was tightening around him as her clit was being vibrated. Suddenly Dave yelled out and started thrusting spasmodically into Kim holding her hips so tight it pinched. Kim could feel her own pressure build to a crescendo and as she contracted she too yelled out with pleasure moving the wand vigorously on her clit whilst she came. They both collapsed as they tried to catch their breath and lay holding each other tenderly as their heart beats were pounding in their chests.

After a few minutes they decided to return to the Jacuzzi to relax and sip their wine. The cold air encased their bodies as they ran into the courtyard, their skin filled with goose bumps. As soon as they were submerged in the hot bubbling water, their bodies were soothed, regaining warmth with a sensation of being wrapped in a warm blanket. They snuggled together in the warm bubbling water looking up at the sky, amazed at the mass of beautiful stars shining so brightly. Out in the valley there was very little artificial light so the stars lit up the sky like a thousand candles. It was certainly very romantic, while they admired the view they sighed pulling each other closer. They lay relaxing and feeling absolutely euphoric as they sipped their wine, regaining their strength. Kim looked into Dave's eyes and said "I love you so much" and Dave replied "I love you more". They kissed softly on the lips, both smiling, feeling very content and safe in each other's arms.

9 EROTIC ENCOUNTERS DINNER IS SERVED

"What do you fancy for dinner tonight? Darling" Sonia texted to Ken, who replied cheekily "you xx". Sonia giggled and playfully replies "OK, would you like me served up hot or cold?" Ken replies "hot, the hotter the better".

Sonia is planning the "dinner" for tonight. She goes shopping to get all of the "goods". On her return she lays out a large plastic sheet on the dining table, lining up everything she is going to need. She has whipping cream, banana, candies, chocolate sauce, bread rolls, and puts a pot of soup on the stove. She then has a shower and puts on her robe.

Sonia hears Ken's car arrive and pull into the garage, she hurriedly runs to meet him at the door. With a beaming smile she gives him a big kiss and hug to welcome him home and says "We are going to have a fun dinner tonight, but you should first go and shower whilst I get everything ready". Ken replied "sounds intriguing" with a smirk on his face. Undoing his tie, he walks into the bedroom. Sonia hears the shower start which is her signal to prepare the "dinner".

She goes around the room closing the blinds so that no one can see in and ensures that the front door is locked. She then takes a mug of soup to the table, cuts the bread roll into chunks and opens up the packets of goodies. This is going to be a work of art to behold, she thought smiling. The mug of soup is placed on the table with the bread chunks placed in a row from the mug to the edge. Sonia slips off her robe and completely naked she climbs onto the table. First she sits to position everything…. the mug of soup she places between her thighs so that she can feel the radiating heat on the inside of her thighs and her love nest. She then takes the can of whipping cream and sprays the outline of panties onto her groin, filling it in with the white creamy foam. She adds chocolate sauce, dribbling it down her love lips.

Next she places three candy jelly snakes on her cream panties, positioned to point down to the love cave. Peeling the banana, she keeps it handy to be poised in her mouth, this will mimic a phallic symbol and what she plans to do to Ken's member. She then lies down and in whipping cream she sprays on a makeshift bikini top, also squirting some onto her nipples to cushion two pink marshmallows, one on each. She hears the bedroom door open, quickly she picks up the banana and places it in her mouth and holds there as Ken walks in.

Ken walks over to the dining table with a big grin on his face and says "well, well, well what do we have here?" Sonia removes the banana from her mouth and says provocatively "Dinner is served" and giggles. Ken walks around the table to scan her artwork. She has a beautiful body and Ken loves how playful she is, never a dull moment with Sonia. She piped up saying "Soup first". Ken walked down to the bottom of the table looked at the mug of soup with the trail of bread chunks between Sonia's legs. He smiled and said "I like hotpot soup" He could see the heat from the soup radiate on Sonia's inner thighs, making them red.

Her love lips which were almost touching the mug were swollen with excitement. Ken dunked a piece of bread into the soup and lifted it above Sonia's belly, letting it dribble into her belly button, which he then slurped up. He dribbled more soup over her belly and watched as it ran down her sides onto the plastic sheet. He used the chunks of bread to mop the soup off her belly and sides, popping it in his mouth he ate it saying "yum". He dribbled a lot more soup over Sonia's belly and with both hands he used the bread chunks to soak it up and eat it as though she was his dining table. Sonia felt the warm soup glide over her belly and trickle down her sides, then the soft fluffy bread being used to soak up the moisture. Ken dunked another piece of bread into the soup and ran it over her toes, the soup dribbled between her toes and down onto her foot. Ken lifted her foot up and sucked her toes clean, it tickled and made Sonia squeal.

Ken removed his robe so as not to get it dirty, standing before Sonia naked and rock hard. Ken walked to the top end of the table where Sonia's head was and leaned over her so that she could suck him. Using the banana, she encircled the tip then took a cheeky bite, giggling. She then took Ken's member into her mouth and started to slowly suck, up and down the shaft whilst cupping his balls in her hand. Leaning forward over Sonia, Ken started to lick around her cream smothered nipples, scooping it up with his tongue before gulping down one of the marshmallows. Using his tongue, he then moved the cream around her nipple, making it slippery, when he started to suck it made Sonia groan. He then moved to the other nipple, sucking in some cream and the other marshmallow. He then pushed her cream laden breasts together making a love tunnel for his member. Pushing through, backwards and forwards, he could feel the soft cream lubricating the way and it really turned him on.

Ken moved to the bottom of the table and removed the mug of soup and remaining bits of bread, this revealed her warm thighs and love nest which were still marked red from the heat. He saw the chocolate sauce that had dribbled down onto her love lips and instantly bent down and started licking the chocolate off, this made Sonia groan with pleasure. He held her hips whilst licking her "cream" panties and in sucking up the whipped cream he captured the candy jelly snakes one by one, dragging them along her love nest and down over her love lips before sucking them into his mouth and chewing on them.

Ken then looked at what other candies were available to play with and noticed chocolate bars. Whilst unwrapping one he exclaimed that he liked chocolate, gliding it down Sonia's love lips, holding it against her love canal he watched it melt from the heat from her excitement. He said "I think the chocolate wants to melt in the love canal" and pushes it into Sonia, making her groan with pleasure as she feels the hard chocolate with smooth creamy liquid melting into her. Ken leaves it sticking out and bends down to suck the melting chocolate that is oozing out mixing with Sonia's warm love juices. Ken pulls out what is left of the bar and pops it into his mouth, then with the chocolate melted over his tongue he licks Sonia's love lips and love canal smearing chocolate over her before licking it off again.

Sonia says, "Your turn" and they switch places. She grabs a candied jelly snake, first dragging it over Ken's torso and then up to his nipples. With the jellied snake she flicks at his nipples making them more erect. Sonia then sprays whipped cream onto his nipples and drags the snakes across them getting them covered in cream. She pops one end of a snake into Ken's mouth whilst having the other end in her own mouth. She chews all the way down to Ken's lips then kisses him passionately. She then suckles on his nipple, sucking it hard, stretching it out as far as it can go, before letting it flick back. She then picked up the chocolate sauce and dribbled some into Ken's belly button before ravenously devouring it. She then took the whipped cream and sprayed it all over Ken's member before taking it into her mouth. As she was gliding up and down, the cream was going into her hair, her face and up her nose. She sprayed cream onto his balls and rubbed her face in it, eating him hungrily, which was driving Ken wild. She then took the chocolate sauce and dribbled it down his shaft, squeezing extra onto the tip of the head. With one hand at the bottom of the shaft, squeezing it tight and the other to twist the shaft and push it into her mouth, so she could suck the head simulating Ken's full length being inside her.

Sonia asked Ken to stand up and as he did she took the mug of soup and dipped his member straight into it. It felt so warm when Sonia put it in her mouth sucking it dry, licking up the last drops. Sonia then told Ken to sit on one of the dining chairs which he did. Sonia straddled him, lowering herself slowly onto Ken's shaft and kissing him passionately to turn on her love tap. Ken could feel how wet Sonia was and pumped into her hard and fast. She was crying out with pleasure when Ken grabbed her bouncing breasts, caressing them he took a nipple into his mouth and sucked it hard which made Sonia flinch and contract around his member. Ken told Sonia to get back up on the table and lie on her back while keeping her bottom towards the edge.

Ken then stood at the end of the table and lifted Sonia's legs straight up against his body placing her feet on either of his shoulders. Each time he plunged deep into Sonia she groaned loudly, he kept pumping for a while before bending her legs back like a frog. He picked up the can of whipping cream and sprayed it on his member which he then pushed into Sonia, each time he pulled out the cream would ooze and smother his member with the white creamy substance. He sprayed the cream onto her clit and started to rub with his thumb. Being moist from the cream enabled the agitation of the clit to be vigorous, this led to Sonia crying out in ecstasy. Ken stopped to savour the moment, he took one of the jellied snakes and pushed it into Sonia with just its head poking out. He then started to bite it, pulling it out with his teeth while taking bites off and chewing the lolly. He could taste her love juice as it mixed with the sweet sugary taste of the candy. Ken asked Sonia to turn over, so she was bent over the table and holding onto both sides. He pushed her legs apart with his foot and taking the chocolate sauce he dribbled it down her back and butt cheeks. He then started to lick all the way up her back which Sonia thought felt sensational, when he was between her butt cheeks, licking the full length, he drove Sonia wild. Her love juices started to flow and she kept pushing her bottom out offering for Ken to be inside her. Ken said "Not yet my darling", then sprayed cream between her butt cheeks and hungrily ate it all up. He kissed her thighs and then her love lips which were so wet. He sucked them dry stretching them out then letting them flick back. Sonia was lying with her head on its side and her groaning was vibrating in her ear.

Ken then circled his member around the love lips, it was almost as though he was vacuuming up the last drops of cream. Sonia kept pushing back onto him to make him enter. Ken slowly pushed himself into Sonia and laid his body down on the back of hers spreading his arms along hers and holding the top of her hands. Gently he thrust in and out, his body weight pinning her to the table. He then stood up and quickened his pace, whilst holding her hips he thrust deeper and deeper going faster and faster. Sonia was crying out; she could feel the pressure build as she contracted around his member. The tightness just made Ken squeeze her hips tighter as he thrust harder and harder into her, then as he started to hit climax he yelled at the top of his voice, jerking spasmodically and emptying himself into her. Sonia was panting as she had cum too, Ken then just slumped down onto her with his heart pounding into her back. They both lay very still gaining their strength and catching their breath. Once recovered they jumped into the shower together, lathered up and washed each other clean before putting on their robes and going out to clear up the mess. As they were picking up all the empty packets and left over foods Ken said "Thank you for dinner, Darling, have to say you have probably become my favourite meal." They both laughed and once the mess was cleaned up they got into bed, held each other close, thinking they were so lucky to have one another.

10 EROTIC ENCOUNTERS ON AN AIRLINE

Mandy was so excited as she had never flown business class before. It was such a wonderful surprise when John revealed the boarding passes to her in the airport club lounge where they were sitting sipping champagne, imagining their holiday to Venice, Italy. It was going to be so romantic walking hand in hand alongside the Grand Canal, being serenaded snuggled up on the gondola and indulging in the Italian cuisine at the many quaint restaurants.

John and Mandy had been dating for two years and this was their first big overseas holiday together. They met through friends and instantly connected. John was a solicitor and Mandy a psychologist, both with a keen passion to help people. It had been a hectic year so they were both in need of a holiday to unwind and relax, and what better place than Italy, the mecca of love.

"Flight 724 is now boarding to Venice from gate 23" came over the tannoy. Mandy and John hurriedly scooped up their belongings and headed toward the gate. As they sat down in their business class seats Mandy was busily exploring the gadgets and settling in to her comfy surrounds for the 9.5-hour flight.

As the flight attendant collected the remains of the dinner service Mandy and John reclined their seats, wine in hand they pulled the blanket over their legs whilst they watched a movie.

Mandy was next to the window, she looked across at John, smiled and proceeded to place her hand under the blanket and searched for the front of his trousers. She slowly unzipped his trousers putting her hand inside his underwear. John lifted his left knee up discreetly so that the other passengers couldn't see what was going on. Mandy slowly caressed his member, it grew in her hand as it received more and more affection. She moved her hand further down, letting her fingernails gently claw his balls, pulling them upwards towards his shaft which made it bounce. John leant across and whispered to Mandy to remove her panties from under her skirt. Mandy, under the protective cloak of the blanket, managed to remove her panties without being seen. John put his hand under the blanket, moving his hand along her thigh. Mandy responded by parting her legs to give him access. John could feel how wet Mandy was, the possibility of being caught always made her so excited. John rubbed Mandy's clit softly and she sighed, closing her eyes. John pushed his finger in and out of Mandy, but it was hard to muffle the noise of the squelching love juice, even under the blanket. John whispered to Mandy "Meet me in the toilet cubicle in one minute"

He got up, pulling his shirt over the top of his pants to hide his protruding member. Mandy waited until she could see that John had gone into the toilet cubicle, she then stood up letting her skirt fall back into its normal position while hiding the fact she was wearing no panties. A couple of taps on the door and Mandy was let into the confined space of the cubicle. They hungrily started to kiss and hurriedly loosened their clothing to gain access to each other. John dropped his trousers and underpants to the floor, putting the lid down on the toilet he sat down. Mandy knelt down on the floor and took John's member into her mouth, she dribbled saliva over it and hungrily lunged herself onto it so that it went deep into her mouth. John held her head gently and pushed into her. Mandy lifted her t-shirt and let her lacy bra rub against his thighs. John said "Let me do you" Mandy stood up, followed by John. He said "stand on the toilet". Mandy climbed onto the toilet and put her hands up onto the ceiling to steady herself as the plane had hit turbulence. John said "turn around and bend over", and Mandy complied. John grabbed her cheeks and lifted them up so he could gain access to her swollen love lips. They were absolutely dripping and John sucked them slurping up the juices. He rubbed his finger on her clit which drove Mandy wild causing John to say shush a few times to remind her of their surroundings so that they wouldn't be disturbed. He grabbed some napkins and said "hold these to your mouth to muffle the sound". The scent of Mandy's musk filled the cubicle, this drove John wild and he kept inhaling deeply as he couldn't get enough of it. He then used all of his fingers to tickle under Mandy, the multiple touches, all at once, was like turning on the tap for more juices to flow down over John's fingers. John pushed his thumb into Mandy to lubricate it, then pulled it out and slowly pushed it into her bottom. Mandy cried out into the napkins which she held tightly against her mouth. John gently and slowly pushed his thumb in and out whilst using his other hand to push two fingers into her love nest, the rhythm pushing in and out in both places was making Mandy groan. She pushed her bottom back towards John to push him deeper.

Mandy so wanted John inside her but wanted to make it last too. Mandy got down off the toilet and sat on it lifting her t-shirt over her head. She undid her bra releasing her breasts, they bounced out of their captivity hardening, looking for his touch. John caressed her breasts, squeezing them with his hands then pulling a nipple into his mouth, sucking it.

112

Meanwhile, Mandy was pulling John's shaft with one hand and caressing his balls with the other. She was squeezing tighter up and down the shaft pinching at the tip to move the skin over his sensitive head. Suddenly she had an idea and reached across to the soap pump to retrieve some soap to help lubricate. She spat into her soapy hand to help it lather up and taking his member back into her hand it glided with ease, soft and smooth, gliding effortlessly up and down.

John began to groan, especially when the soap suds collected at the tip making it extra sensitive. Mandy pumped more soap out of the dispenser, this time smearing it over and between her breasts. She pulled John closer, placing her breasts either side of John's member, pulling her breast together and tightly encasing his member in the cocoon of love. John thrust between Mandy's breasts, with the soapy suds it slipped up and down with ease and felt amazing. He held her shoulders to stabilise himself whilst she held her breasts together so that he could thrust between them. John was groaning with pleasure and it was Mandy's turn to say shush to remind him where they were. Mandy bent her head over to face her breasts, sticking out her tongue, so each time John's tip burst through the love canal it hit Mandy's tongue which was so warm, soft and moist. John thrust harder to ensure he pushed up against her tongue with each thrust. John knew he was getting close and had to stop. He wanted to get Mandy close too so that they could cum together.

John asked Mandy to stand back up on the toilet and bend over in front of him holding her ankles. He then started to kiss her swollen lips gently, flicking his tongue on her clitoris. He slipped two fingers into her, hooked them around so he was applying pressure to her G spot. He started to massage her G spot whilst using his other hand to rub her clit. This was driving Mandy wild, love juices were flowing down her thighs and she was groaning with delight. John couldn't help it, but with her smooth bottom before him, he literally wanted to eat her and clenched his teeth into her cheek. Mandy flinched and her muscles contracted clenching his fingers inside her. John knew she was close and asked her to get down and stand facing the door whilst he sat down on the toilet.

Mandy lowered herself down onto John as she steadied herself with one hand on the basin and the other against the wall. John was as hard as a rock and she could feel him fill her to capacity, his entry eased by her natural juices. Mandy with bent knees hovered above John so he could thrust up into her, she struggled to stay quiet as each thrust made her gasp with pleasure. John held her waist tight to keep her in position as she held the basin tight. Each thrust went deep and her juices dripped onto John's thighs. As he pushed in and out, he pulled Mandy down onto him and pushed her back up again. John's pace started to quicken, he was thrusting so hard that the whole cubicle was vibrating. The pressure started to build and John could feel Mandy tighten around him. John started convulsing, going deep with his body jerking, as he groaned loudly. Mandy felt John burst into her, it was like hot lava. She could feel herself clenching John's member tight as he continued to thrust until she came. They were both groaning loudly and crying out in pleasure until they slumped fully spent. Both having totally forgotten where they were, they wondered how they were going to be received leaving the cubicle together. They quickly cleaned themselves up and got dressed. Mandy said there was no way she was going out first, she pushed John close to the door so that his tall stature could shadow her embarrassment behind him. They walked gingerly back to their seats receiving disgusted looks from most of the passengers. One man winked in admiration, wishing he and his wife had the courage to do that.

They sat down in their seats, snuggled up, still connecting as one and holding each other close. They pulled the blanket over them, secretly wishing it was a blanket of invisibility, concealing them from the view of other passengers. They soon dropped off to sleep.

They were awakened by the captain's voice over the tannoy advising they were starting their descent into Venice. They had collected their bags from the carousal when their taxi whisked them away to their hotel, which was alongside the Grand Canal. When they walked into their room, Mandy gasped at the opulence, it was breathtaking. With marble floors, a four poster bed and when she opened the shutters, there was a magnificent view over the Grand Canal. As Mandy swung around John was there to catch her in his arms and he said "I have ordered us some champagne so we can shower then laze in our robes and relax". Mandy took his face in her hands and kissed him passionately, she loved this man so much, he thought of everything.

Mandy went to have a shower, she needed to wash away the long flight and be refreshed and ready to start her romantic holiday with the man she truly loved with all her heart. Stripped of all her clothes she stepped into the shower, the water felt lovely and warm on her skin. She lathered up the soap and started to wash all over her body. The door of the shower opened and there stood John, naked he stepped in to join her. He said "champagne has arrived my darling". Mandy squealed with excitement and lathered the soap in her hands and started to massage John's back. He was tense and she pressed deeper to release the tension in his muscles, slowly she let her hands glide down his back following the trail of soap suds trickling down between his butt cheeks. She ran her fingers between his cheeks and underneath him. He parted his legs so she could gain access and she caressed his balls, running her fingernails through the hair tickling him. John's member started to grow and Mandy turned him around to face her, she knelt down taking John into her mouth, dribbling down the shaft to lubricate as she glided up and down. The water from the shower was trickling down her face and John could feel the warm water wash over his shaft each time Mandy sucked back up to the tip. She stood up facing the wall and placed her feet apart with her hands against the wall above her head. John stood behind her and reached under her to feel how moist she was and rubbed her clit to increase the flow. John pulled Mandy's hips back towards him so she was slightly bent over in front of him and he thrust inside her which made her cry out. She loved it when he entered her with his member without any foreplay, as she is at her tightest and could feel him stretch her to capacity. John thrust deep into Mandy as she pushed herself back onto him. The thrusting was so forceful her breasts were bouncing around uncontrollably. John moved Mandy so that she stood alongside the wall, he could then lift her leg up high around his waist and he could thrust up under her. Mandy was groaning with pleasure as John was thrusting deep into her almost pinning her to the wall, disarming her leg so she couldn't escape. John then stopped and suggested they move into the bedroom.

They towel dried themselves quickly and went into the bedroom to the four poster bed. John used the netting hanging from the posts as a make shift tie to tie Mandy's hands to the bed post, above her head. John then pushed Mandy's legs apart so he could get between them and suck at her swollen love lips and flick his tongue on her clit. Mandy writhed in pleasure groaning. John held her hips, licking and sucking the love juices that were trickling out. John lifted Mandy's legs up around his waist and thrust up into her making her squeal. He could feel how soaking wet she was as her juices started to ooze onto his thighs. John untied her hands and moved her onto the bed saying "go on top". John then lay flat on his back with his member rock hard, he held it at its base so it was at attention, pointing to the ceiling. Mandy straddled him, lowering herself onto his member gasping with pleasure. She started to ride John, up and down really slowly to accentuate his length, she then quickened her pace. John grabbed Mandy's bouncing breasts and reached up to suck her fully erect nipple as he caressed her hard full breasts. John loved Mandy being on top. He enjoyed seeing her breasts bounce before him and feel himself go deep into her as she took his full length. John started to thrust up into Mandy and he could feel the pressure build. He reached his thumb over to rub Mandy's clit whilst thrusting into her, he could feel her tighten around him. Mandy started to groan and they could both feel the crescendo building; they were both riding the waves of passion at high speed. Suddenly John let out a huge cry, still pumping spasmodically as Mandy cried out, panting heavily. Both then slumped, Mandy lay down forward onto John's body and both were breathing heavily with their hearts pounding. Falling asleep, they remained snuggled together until the early morning.

11 Erotic Encounters With a Sheik

Jenny's global company offered her an amazing opportunity to work in the Middle East, an assignment for 6 months. She had always had a fascination with the Middle East and couldn't wait to immerse herself in the culture. As soon as Jenny got off the plane in Dubai she felt a sense of mystique and enchantment.

As soon as Jenny had checked in to her apartment, showered and unpacked she was eager to explore the local bazaar. As she wandered down the narrow streets she could hear the chanting, the call to prayer, for the men to pray at the local mosques. Lots of men could be seen scurrying to the mosque to pray. The heat was quite intense, Jenny walked into a café that had traditional rugs on the floor, huge cushions to sit on and flowing Bedouin curtains. It was like stepping back into an ancient time. Jenny ordered a cool drink and some fruit then sat on a cushion which was situated under a huge fan.

A lot of people would stare at Jenny, she was a beautiful woman with long flowing blonde hair and gorgeous blue eyes. A sight that wasn't seen very often in this part of the world, where everyone had black hair and dark eyes. Jenny dressed conservatively to be respectful wearing long sleeves and long trousers. As she sat sipping her cool drink, she closed her eyes and relaxed, listening to the noise of the swirling fan.

An Arabic man walked into the café, he noticed Jenny sitting alone and asked her if he could sit next to her. Jenny looked up, mesmerised by the brilliant white of the man's robe, in contrast to his dark complexion, dreamy dark eyes and dashing smile. Jenny instantly said "sure, no problem". The man said "My name is Khalil, I am fascinated by your beauty. Your hair is golden like the sand of the dessert and your eyes are as blue as the water hole in an oasis." Jenny blushed and said "Thank you." He asked her if she had been to the desert before and she said "no". He then asked if he could take her, and as it is most beautiful at sunset, they could have supper under the stars. Jenny ordinarily wouldn't go off with a stranger, especially not in a foreign country, but there was something about Khalil that made her feel warm, safe and romantic.

They walked out to an awaiting limousine, Khalil instructed the driver to take them to a destination she was unaware of but pictured it being an amazing and exotic location. About an hour out of the city, they pulled up to a place where some camels were tied. Khalil got out, opened Jenny's door taking her by the hand. He led her to the camels saying that they needed to go the rest of the way by camel. Jenny was so excited, she had never been on a camel before. The camel was sitting down and she was helped up to sit on the woven rug which was a makeshift saddle. Khalil got onto his camel and two men led each camel by the reins into the desert. After about an hour, from the top of a sand dune they looked down to where there was a large tent with a fire ablaze and food being cooked. As they descended the dune the others at the camp greeted Khalil warmly and he introduced Jenny to them. After a hearty meal sitting around the campfire, Jenny looked across at Khalil admiring his features. He was a handsome man and had been so gentlemanly and respectful to her. He could sense her stare and he turned and smiled at her. The fire had started to simmer as the others cleared up and started their travels home. Khalil's and Jenny's camels were tethered to a date palm.

Khalil was showing Jenny the mass of stars that illuminated the night sky in the desert as there are no artificial lights to dim their brightness. They looked so beautiful, Jenny was in awe at the view. She felt Khalil gently pull her closer to him, she looked into his face and he held her head with his hands and softly kissed her. Jenny felt weak at the knees and melted under his charm. Khalil walked her to the tent which was decorated with rugs, cushions and flowing colourful netting which hung from the roof making it look like an exotic Bedouin camp.

Khalil started to unbutton Jenny's shirt which exposed her lacy white lingerie and toned body. He slipped the shirt off her shoulders admiring her body with its porcelain white soft skin. He unzipped her trousers and let them drop to the floor. Her panties were white lace exposing her buttocks as the g string sat snug between her cheeks. Jenny stepped out of her trousers and stood in her lingerie before Khalil, who walked around her to admire her whole body. Khalil removed his head scarf, and then slowly lifted off his white robe. Jenny was surprised, as he wasn't wearing anything underneath. Khalil was golden brown, muscular and very masculine. He was already showing signs of excitement as his arousal could be seen growing.

Khalil led Jenny over to the bathing area and he took a towel, soaked it in the warm water fragranced with jasmine and gently washed her body. Moving the towel over her smooth skin he watched her goose bumps rise especially as he moved across her hardened nipples. Khalil continued all over her body as though he was exploring every inch of her form. Once finished she was to do the same for him. She picked up a fresh towel, soaked it and moved it over his body, watching it glisten with moisture she relished, taking in his beauty as she explored his body. He was fully erect when she put the towel down and knelt before him, softly licking the tip of his member which flicked with excitement. She cupped her hand under him and gently massage his balls, she could feel him harden as she took him into her mouth and slowly dribbled saliva along his shaft. One hand was massaging up and down the shaft as she sucked the throbbing head in and out, whilst the other hand gently squeezed his balls, both hands moving in rhythm. Khalil collected her hair into a ponytail which he held tightly bringing her head back and forth to glide her along his shaft with her mouth. He tightened his grip and thrust into her throat a few times making her gag which brought tears to her eyes. He immediately regained composure, loosened his grip on her hair and with his left hand wiped the tear that had escaped down her cheek. He lifted her up by her hand and walked her over to the cushions. He stacked two large cushions on top of each other and beckoned Jenny to lie over the top of them midway so that her bottom protruded into the air.

Khalil got some oil that smelled like sandalwood, he poured it along the middle of Jenny's back and dribbled it between her cheeks. He then started to massage Jenny with his strong hands, first across her shoulders and then moving down to her lower back kneading her muscles, making her feel so relaxed and warm. He started to massage the oil across her butt cheeks in circular motions, allowing the side of his hand to slip between her butt cheeks, gliding softly, lubricated by the oil. He continued to run his hand between her butt cheeks then moving further underneath her, lubricating her love nest which was already moist from her own love juices in anticipation of their love making. The sensual circling of his strong hands over her bottom and down underneath her sliding with the warm oil was so arousing.

Jenny was arched over the cushions with her bottom exposed when Khalil spread her legs and knelt behind her. With both hands he clutched her butt cheeks and pushed his hard member into her love nest, Jenny let out a cry of pleasure as he pushed himself deep into her. He withdrew very slowly until just the tip was inside before plunging deeply into her again, making Jenny cry out. She gripped the cushions tightly with her hands as Khalil played this slow and fast game showing he was in control of her pleasure. As he plunged deep into her he slapped her butt cheek hard, this made Jenny flinch and contract around his shaft. Khalil lay his body on top of her oiled back and let his arms lie along her arms as if holding her down and in place. He continued to thrust in and out as Jenny groaned with pleasure. He then got up and picked up the tails of the flowing Bedouin curtains and asked Jenny to turn over. He wrapped the tail of a curtain around each of Jenny's hands as she lay with her arms outstretched above her head, her back arched over the cushions and her love mound raised high above her thighs. Khalil moved back to Jenny and lifted her legs up to his standing body, he then wrapped her legs around his waist. He once again plunged deep inside of Jenny, holding her hips he pulled her onto him as he pushed hard into her. Jenny was crying out in pleasure, her love juices flowing down her butt cheeks and dripping onto the rugs. Khalil gathered the central tent curtain tails which were hanging above his head. He pulled on them to release so that he could tie Jenny's feet together and hoist her up. Her love lips, swollen and glistening, were at chest height for him. Khalil licked her love lips which made Jenny groan with delight. He couldn't get enough of her juices, he pushed his fingers into her allowing the juices to flow as he slurped them up. Jenny was wriggling but couldn't escape, with her legs and arms bound she was captured for his delight. He was in control of her pleasure.

Khalil walked behind Jenny's head and knelt on all fours, leaning over her, with his manhood pushing against her mouth. As her hands were tied, Jenny was reliant on him guiding himself into her mouth, he thrust his member into her mouth gently so as not to hurt her. He sucked her nipple and as she sucked him he could feel the vibrations of her groans along his shaft. He caressed her breast, cupping it in his hand as he sucked the nipple, extending it and tugging it between his teeth until it could stretch no further. The more he tugged the nipple, the more Jenny groaned and tightened the grip on his shaft with her mouth. He moved to her other breast and did the same, this time using his other hand to find her love mound and rub her oiled clitoris which was erect with excitement. As he rubbed her clit Jenny groaned even more and wriggled to heighten her own pleasure. Khalil sucked her nipple and rubbed her clit as he thrust into her mouth. The more pleasure he gave her instantly gave him pleasure too as her mouth would tighten around him and her groans were vibrating up his shaft.

Khalil got up and walked back to where Jenny's legs were bound. He loosened each curtain tail but tightened the curtain on each foot, sending her legs apart. He tied both curtains off leaving Jenny spread eagled, arms and legs, for him to take her. Khalil held Jenny's hips as he stood between her legs and he slowly entered her. Gliding in and out very slowly, he drove Jenny crazy. He rubbed his thumb on her clit and she was crying out in pleasure, her juices were trickling out as she tightened around him. Khalil increased the pace, holding her hips tight so that he could plunge deep into her. Jenny was crying out with pleasure as he continued to thrust hard into her. He stopped, pulled out and bent down to suck her clit, she screamed out as it was now so hyper sensitive. He then got up and again pushed himself into her, thrusting fast and hard. He could feel he wasn't going to last too much longer but he wanted to make sure that Jenny came at the same time. He stopped again, pulled out and sucked her clit. Jenny was thrusting into his face, she was ready. Khalil held her hips tight and thrust fast and hard into her, they could both feel the pressure building until they screamed out with their bodies convulsing. As Khalil pumped his last drops into her, they collapsed, fully spent. Khalil was dripping with sweat and panting for breath. Jenny too was breathing hard still clinging onto the curtains.

At that moment, Jenny tried to untangle herself from the curtain but couldn't and suddenly woke up. She found herself in the café in a tangle from the curtains that had been blown by the fan, large cushions across her feet which weighed her down. She looked around and could see people were looking at her, clearly wondering what on earth she was doing. She blushed as she wondered to what extent had she played out her erotic dream whilst asleep on the floor of the café.

Jenny quickly untangled herself, giggled and bade farewell to the café audience.

12 Erotic Encounters Dominatrix

Today started out like any normal day, except today Kylie was feeling more assertive, confident and sensual. She felt like dressing up, but not in her usual way. She went to the wardrobe and pulled out her secret bag of sexy clothes selecting a black leather corset, black lacy lingerie, stockings and heels. Opening her toy box she took out all the "toys" she wanted to play with on Tom tonight. The excitement started to tingle in her body as she thought about what she wanted to do to Tom when he got home.

After soaking in a bubble bath, Kylie scattered candles around the bedroom and closed the blinds. She sent Tom a text advising him not to be late or there would be consequences. Tom laughed when he read the text because he knew what a night he was going to be in for and his groin started to ache with anticipation. Tom loved it when Kylie took charge in the bedroom, it made him feel so vulnerable, so submissive and so overpowered, just what a guy needs every now and then he thought laughing.

Kylie heard the key in the front door, she walked over grabbing the handle before Tom could make his way in, she was the authority on whether he could enter or not. She stood before him dressed in her black corset, which hugged her body tight and pushed her breasts up creating a deep cleavage. Her lacy black lingerie, black stockings and high heels heightened the feminine sensuality that Kylie oozed. Kylie said "Hello Darling, I hope you're not too tired from your day at work." Tom replied, "I'm never too tired for you my love" and kissed her softly on the lips holding her face in his hands. Kylie led him to the bedroom which was candlelit, the flames flickered from the breeze they created when walking in.

Tom sees the rope tied to the bed post and some of Kylie's "toys" lined up on the bedside table, he starts to tingle all over in anticipation. Kylie starts to unbutton his shirt, she kisses his chest whilst hovering her palms over his nipples touching them ever so softly, which makes them erect. As her hands gently peel his shirt from his shoulders she runs her fingernails back over his chest and down his torso, leaving red welts. She reaches his trousers and undoes his fly letting them drop to the floor, she taps his foot with her stiletto to suggest he step out of his trousers, as he does she flicks them across the room with her shoe. She bends down and kisses his stomach then moves to his upper thighs, she sees his member grow inside his underwear, she slides them down allowing his member to bounce out, erect, like a jack in the box. To heighten the anticipation, she blows soft warm air up and down the shaft without touching.

Kylie tells Tom to move onto the bed and get down on all fours as she reaches for the massage oil. She dribbles some down the arch of his back and over his butt cheeks. Kneeling next to him she starts to massage his back, sliding up and down, applying pressure but not too much. She lets her hands move over Tom's butt cheeks, massaging them softly, allowing oil to seep down between his cheeks and dribble right down to his scrotum. With her finger she traces the dribbling oil between his cheeks, pushing against his skin and down to his sack and starts to massage the oil into his balls. Whilst her hands glide effortlessly she is mindful not to touch his shaft that is throbbing hard and searching for her touch.

She runs her oiled finger gently back up between his cheeks and pushes it into his cavity, Tom lets out a cry of pleasure and pain. As she gently pushes her oiled finger deeper into him, his hands clench the sheets and the pressure rises against his prostate sending sensations up his entire shaft. She moves her finger slowly in and out, allowing his muscles to relax and with her other hand she glides the length of his shaft, moving in time with the pressure being pushed inside him. He groans loudly. Kylie grabs a butt plug, lathers it with oil, then slowly pushes it inside Tom who shrieks with the pressure and pain being induced. Kylie holds the butt plug in place whilst caressing his shaft which helps to relax his muscles.

Kylie gets two pieces of rope and ties the ends to two bed posts. She then ties an ankle to a piece of rope and does the same with the other ankle to the opposite best post. She pulls the rope taut which draws his legs towards the opposing bed posts, spreading his legs apart. She then ties his hands together above his head and pushes his shoulders down onto the bed. His bottom is sticking up in the air, his hands and knees tied into position allowing her to do as she pleases. All of a sudden Tom feels a slap of leather tassels whip across his back, as he yells out another lashing occurs leaving welts on his back. Kylie says, "Have you been bad Tom?" and Tom answers "yes I have been bad Kylie". Kylie replies "How bad have you been Tom?" and Tom answers "Very bad, Kylie." Kylie responds with a whip across his bottom shouting "I thought so". Tensing his muscles, Tom shrieks in pain and loses his erection due to the pain. He was still maintaining hold of the butt plug which was deeply embedded in his bottom. Everything went quiet, and then he could hear something that sounded like metal. Kylie had reached down and encased Tom's member and balls into a metal barred cage, locking it closed. It held Tom's soft member and balls tightly inside.

"Now you do remember the safe word don't you Tom?" asked Kylie to which Tom replied "yes, moonshine." Kylie ran her fingernails up the back of Tom's thighs, digging them in hard, leaving red lines up his legs. Tom flinched, every time he received pain his muscles would tense, including those clutching the butt plug, which would induce more pain. Kylie then flicked the whip tassels over Tom's bottom and his scrotum, which was still captured in the cage, this made him flinch more. Kylie then kissed his red welted bottom tenderly, digging her teeth in just enough to inflict slight pain, this made Tom jump and in turn contract his muscles inflicting even more pain in his bottom. Kylie then picked up a feather and started to tickle through the bars of the metal cage which encased Tom's genitals and he started to wriggle. Kylie grabbed hold of the cage with her hand and blew warm breath through the bars which made Tom groan with pleasure. Through the bars she flicked her tongue at his genitals, Tom could feel little flicks but suddenly felt her suck in some of his ball sack and stretch it through the bars of the cage. This made Tom groan as he could feel himself being stretched and his member respond, it was trying to push up against the cage to find a way out, but it was locked.

Kylie moved to the other side of the bed to where Tom could face her. She then lifted one heeled foot up onto the bed and slowly unclipped the suspender belt, she rolled down her stocking and slipped off her shoe discarding them onto the floor. She then lifted her other foot onto the bed, unclipped the suspender belt and removed that stocking and shoe. She then slid her panties off revealing her moist love lips. As she undid her corset, which released her breasts, they came bouncing out of their constricted vice. Kylie then proceeded to lie down in front of Tom's face with her vibrator, she rubbed it up and down her swollen love lips and started moaning. Tom wriggled to try and reach her but with his hands tied and his feet firmly locked into their roped position at the bed posts, on the other side of the bed, this was not possible. Kylie slowly put the vibrator inside herself gliding in and out and groaning, this was driving Tom mad as he frantically wanted to join in on the action. She continued to play with herself, he could hear the squelching of her love juices and her groans of pleasure. His member tried to grow but had nowhere to expand to within the cage. Tom could feel the pressure build as the bars on the cage started to dig into his shaft and constrict his balls.

Kylie had started to rub her clit with her other hand whilst pushing the vibrator in and out. She then pushed the button to make it vibrate and started to groan more and more as she thrust into the vibrator to push it deeper. Tom was groaning in pain as his genitals were bursting against the bars of the cage which were now pinching his skin. Tom was shouting out "It's really hurting now" and Kylie kept on pleasuring herself, even taking her clit finger and sucking it into her mouth to lubricate it and return to rubbing her clit. Tom was going red in the face and breathing heavily as his member was getting very hard pinned up against the metal cage. Kylie then removed the vibrator, shifting her pelvis until it was under Tom's face and he ravenously starting to suck at her love lips like he was in a feeding frenzy, starved of food. With his hands still tied he could only manoeuvre his head, he kept sucking to gain some grip on her grabbing at her love lips, her clit and even her inner thighs with his mouth trying to drag her closer. Kylie inched closer and grabbed his head to guide him. She was oozing with love juices in the excitement of seeing Tom restricted and trying to eat her ravenously. Tom was enjoying the feast so much that his member was being crushed, inducing severe pain, making Tom yell out "moonshine, moonshine, moonshine, hurry get this damn thing off me" Kylie jumped up quick and unlocked the cage letting Tom's member jump out like a jack in the box, bright red from being constricted. Tom cried out as the blood returned to his member, like a limb that had gone to sleep, he felt searing pain as pins and needles set in. Kylie started to kiss it tenderly, all the way up the shaft, licking it as though licking a wound. Circling the tip of the shaft with her tongue before taking him fully into her mouth, sliding up and down softly and slowly, soothing the pain. She then untied his ankles and hands so he could be free to take her. Tom was so aroused; it was like he was a lion let out of its cage after been constantly teased by onlookers.

He grabbed Kylie and threw her on the bed making her squeal. He dragged her to the edge of the bed and knelt, lifting her thighs up before hungrily licking and sucking her swollen lips and clit making Kylie groan with pleasure. She grabbed his head, pulling him closer to her and pushing him into her love nest. He couldn't wait any longer and stood up clutching her legs up his torso he plunged deep into her making her cry out. He thrust harder and harder, faster and faster groaning like a mad man. Kylie started to rub her clit as she could see Tom was ready to explode and she could feel herself contract tightly around him. Tom could see Kylie's breasts jiggling around before him, he stops and grabs them both in his hands, sucking the nipples hungrily, alternating from one to the other. He then flips her over and tells her to go on all fours with her knees at the edge of the bed. Plunging deep into Kylie she yells out as he stretches her to full capacity. Tom kept thrusting harder and faster like there was no tomorrow. As his grip tightened on her hips, she vigorously rubbed her clit to ensure she came at the same time as she knew Tom was on the brink. All of a sudden Tom explodes with a huge groan, gripping her thighs so tightly he was pinching them. Kylie too felt the pressure build, pushing back onto Tom as she felt the waves of orgasm carry her away with pleasure. She then cries out arching her back sending him deeper. They collapse, panting and totally spent. They lay on their backs on the bed. Kylie lay with her head on Tom's arm whilst his other arm was draped across her body and he could feel her heartbeat pounding under his arm. They both try to catch their breath and then suddenly Kylie says "Now don't you be bad again", and they both burst out laughing and kissed each other on the lips. Tom said "Geez I love you, even though you do nearly kill me" and flopped back down on the bed.

13 Erotic Encounters Hidden Surprise

Chris pulled up in his van to pick Amy up for their date. He looked very handsome, with a sparkle in his eye and a beaming smile. His shirt was taut against his lean tanned body and Amy could feel her heart quicken. It was a chilly night and Amy wore her long black & white woollen coat that clung to her figure. Little did Chris know that she had nothing on underneath. Just the thought of being naked under her coat was making Amy so horny, it was as though she was wearing an invisible cloak that no one could see what she was hiding. Amy could feel that she was getting wet and was worried it would drip onto her coat as she sat down in the car. Amy leant across and gave Chris a long slow and passionate kiss, just to tease him for what was to come.

They started to drive across the bridge, before heading down the winding roads to the bay, for dinner and drinks at the waterfront pub. As Chris drove, Amy reached across and unzipped his trousers, it took him by surprise but he didn't resist. Amy reached into his underpants to find that he had already started to grow with anticipation. Amy took his member out, leant across and dribbled saliva all down its shaft. Amy moved her hand up the shaft which glided with ease, the saliva acting like lubricant. Amy circled the head with her fingertip then bent over to take him into her mouth. Chris lifted his arm off the steering wheel to give her access and Amy took him into her mouth, slowly gliding up and down, going deeper with each downward motion. Chris started to groan as he lovingly stroked her hair but he had to also focus on the road. Amy sucked tighter as she went up and down then with her tongue she flicked the tip. Amy could feel Chris getting rock hard and her own love juices starting to flow. Amy thought that was sufficient as an entrée to their love making later so she pulled back, putting Chris's attire back as it was.

Amy reached across, held Chris's hand and felt so close to him on another level. They pulled up in the car park and as soon as Chris had turned off the engine he reached across and kissed Amy passionately, with such force it made her groan with pleasure. They forced themselves apart, they wanted to savour the sexual tension in order to drive each other crazy and to explode with ecstasy later. They walked into the pub hand in hand and sat down at a table overlooking the water. They ordered their food and a drink to ease into the ambience of the romantic scene. They sat very close together and could feel the heat of their bodies merge. Amy took out her phone, scrolled to an app "Pretty

Love" and whispered to Chris to activate it. As soon as he did, it sent shudders through Amy's womanhood. The love egg she had inserted before she left home vibrated intensely. Amy let out a cry and grabbed Chris's arm tight, the sensation was riveting and caused her juices to flow freely. Amy told Chris what was happening to her, that she was wearing a love egg and was naked under her coat, he couldn't believe it. His eyes nearly popped out of his head but he was beaming with a great big smile at what they were doing out in public, unbeknownst to everyone around them.

Chris revelled in having the control of Amy's pleasure via her phone. He moved it away from her so he could be in control to trigger the vibrations. He switched it off and they continued to snuggle and chat. Their food came and they started to eat when all of a sudden the vibrations shook Amy, she let out a squeal, in shock, as didn't know it was coming. Chris burst out laughing as he was the master of her ecstasy. The love juices were really flowing and Amy was worried it would flood through her coat for everyone to see when she stood up. As soon as they had finished their meal and drink, it was decided that they needed to go as they really couldn't keep their hands off each other any longer. Amy stood up gingerly, due to the amount of lubricating fluids that were flowing she was half expecting the egg to slide out. Amy could feel a trickle down her inner thighs and told Chris they need to hurry. They walked to the car as fast but as carefully as possible. Chris started the car as well as triggering the vibrations, this made Amy squeal again and they kissed each other hungrily. They drove off so they could get home to start their wild lovemaking.

As they got home and walked into the house, Chris pushed Amy up against the wall pinning her there with the weight of his body, kissing her passionately whilst holding her face in his hands. He started to unbutton her long coat to reveal her warm naked body, the glistening juices down her thighs could be seen in the faint light. He ushered Amy into the bedroom and slipped her coat off before laying her back on the bed. He opened her legs to see she was flooded with juices which he started to slurp up hungrily. He licked up and down her thighs then licking her love lips and clit that were soaking wet. He sucked her clitoris which made her groan with pleasure before triggering the egg to vibrate that sent her wild. Chris removed his clothes whilst he watched Amy's body writhing on the bed in ecstasy. As he dropped his underpants to the floor she could see he was as hard as a rock, she wanted him to make love to her but he dropped to his knees and with his teeth tugged the love egg tail to ease it out. It was hard to pull at first, as she was clenched tightly around it, but with the help of the love juices it then slipped out quickly, dripping with fluid.

Chris reached for her toy box, he pulled out the blindfold to put on Amy's face then the rope to tie her hands together above her head. Amy couldn't see so didn't know what was going to happen next, this heightened her excitement, she could feel her nipples were erect in anticipation and her womanhood was literally aching for him to enter her. Chris wanted to slow things down, he wanted to make their night of passion last. Amy could feel his warm body hovering over her when she suddenly felt a nipple sucked into his mouth with such force it made Amy arch her back and groan. He used his palm to glide across the other nipple very slowly and lightly to tease it. Amy could feel his heavy breath which was exciting her more. He then kissed her passionately, gliding his hand down her torso to her womanhood which was so wet it felt as if it was begging for him to enter. He moved down the bed and then he licked the length of her womanhood in strokes up and down, flicking his tongue on her clitoris which made her squirm with delight. He pulled her legs to the edge of the bed so her bottom was right on the edge, he then lifted her legs so he could thrust his tongue deep into her, whilst holding her thighs in place to stop her from moving. Amy was crying out with pleasure as he continued to lunge his tongue into her, slurping up the juices and sucking at the love lips and clitoris to mop up any remaining flow. He was now exploring putting his fingers into her allowing the juices to trickle between them before sucking them dry. She could feel movement on the bed but didn't know where he was going when all of a sudden his manhood was being pushed into her mouth. Amy started to suck it but as her hands were tied she could not hold it, she had to manoeuvre her head to keep it in place. Chris continued to fondle her in the 69 position, pushing his fingers slowly in and out then slurping the juices as they flowed out after his fingers.

Amy asked Chris to untie her and take the blindfold off so she could pleasure him. She got him to lie on his back on the bed then blindfolded him and tied his hands above his head. He could now just hear and feel but could not see. He heard her footsteps leave the room and wondered what was happening as he could then hear banging and clanging in the kitchen. Amy came back into the room and told him to get on all fours on the bed, still blindfolded with his hands tied. As he did so, she got her accessories ready. As soon as he was in place Amy took an ice cube and ran it up his inner thigh to his scrotum, circling around and around, Chris flinching. With his manhood hanging down between his legs, Amy lifted a cup and dunked his member into warm water which shocked Chris as the ice cube still was encircling his scrotum. The opposite temperatures played tricks with his senses. Amy then switched and dunked his balls into the cup of warm water whilst she slowly ran the ice cube up his shaft. Chris wriggled and Amy told him to stay still.

He could hear the crackling of paper as Amy opened a toy to use on him. It was a finger length mini vibrator which she lubricated by putting inside her then taking it out she slowly eased it into Chris's bottom. Because of the size he thought it was her finger but once fully inserted she pushed the button which made it come to life, vibrating inside Chris. Chris yelled in ecstasy and jerked as it started and Amy again told him to stay still. He could feel the vibrations on the back of his prostrate before they travelled up the shaft of his manhood. It was mind blowing. Amy allowed this sensation for no more than 5 minutes to avoid him coming. She then removed the vibrator, untied him and took the blindfold off. They were both so hot with Amy still throbbing for his manhood to enter her, they couldn't wait any longer. Chris pushed Amy onto her back, pulling her to the edge of the bed, he then lifted her legs up the length of his body before plunging deep inside her and they both let out a huge groan of pleasure. Chris was thrusting harder and faster, tightly holding her legs in place. Her breasts were jiggling as each thrust went through her body. Amy could feel him filling her to capacity, going deeper and deeper, it was driving her wild. Chris stopped abruptly, pushed two fingers into her, then vigorously rubbed them on her G spot and she could feel the pressure building. He then plunged his member into her again thrusting harder and faster before pulling out and pushing his fingers in again rubbing her G spot, vibrating with his hand really fast. Amy could feel the pressure gaining momentum, she just wanted to cum and reached down to touch her clitoris, Chris said "no, leave it".

He plunged into her again going really fast, Amy was crying out with pleasure when he pulled out and pushed his fingers in and found her G spot vibrated it with his hand. She could feel the crescendo of pressure build, grinding her teeth she felt the pressure explode out of her as she squirted all over Chris's legs. As Amy was screaming out, Chris plunged his face into her womanhood to slurp up the flow as she was panting and convulsing, her body twitching in ecstasy. Chris stood up plunged himself into her and went very hard and fast until he climaxed, screaming out with pleasure, he jerked spasmodically into her until he was spent. He collapsed onto her and they held each other, panting and smiling, as they connected on another level bathing in euphoria.

14 EROTIC ENCOUNTERS THREESOME

Chelsea was intrigued when her husband, John suggested they have a threesome with Greg. After all these years their sex life needed some excitement and she had always had a secret crush on Greg, John's best friend. Chelsea said that she didn't want to do it at home, they must hire a hotel room to fulfil this fantasy. John didn't care where they did it as long as it happened, he was thrilled that she agreed. John said "I know Greg will be up for it, he hasn't been out with a woman since his breakup with Mary which is over a year ago. It will do him good to have fire in his belly again." John called Greg, who was up for it, and they discussed the details.

Over the weekend Chelsea went to the local store to buy some lingerie for this special occasion. She picked out a burgundy set that was lacy and very feminine and bought a suspender belt and stockings to match. She went to the hairdressers to have her beautiful long blonde curly hair done. Next, she decided to go all out to have some waxing done, eyebrows, under arms, legs….and you know where else……yep you guessed it……. Brazilian! Chelsea felt amazing as she hopped into the car and headed home.

That evening she started to get ready, she put the lingerie on with stockings and high heels, even she had to admit she looked hot. Over this she wore her sexy black dress that hugged her figure. Chelsea then headed down to the car alone, as she was meeting John and Greg at the hotel. Driving along she felt so excited about what lay ahead and started to fantasise. She could feel her groin tingling in anticipation.

She pulled into the carpark of the hotel and texted John, asking for the room number. He texted back room 202. Chelsea walked through the foyer confidently, heads turned to see this beautiful woman stride through to the elevators. Chelsea went up to the second floor and knocked on the door. John opened the door, he looked so handsome, he had had his hair cut, bought a new shirt and trousers and a very nice cologne. John took her by the hand and kissed her softly saying "you look so beautiful darling." John led Chelsea into the lounge to where Greg was standing, he had a toned body and looked very handsome. Chelsea looked around, she was shocked to see some contraption on the bedroom door and asked "what on earth is that?" Greg answered, "It's a sex swing". Chelsea felt tingles running up her back as she imagined making love whilst being straddled in the swing. John offered champagne and once all three were charged with a glass and had had a few sips, Greg said "shall we take our drinks into the bedroom"? They entered the bedroom where there was a king size bed.

They all started to undress, Chelsea stripped down to her lingerie and stood before the men, who both complimented her on how hot she looked. The men had stripped right off, both eager to get into the action. They told Chelsea to lie on the bed. John proceeded to kiss Chelsea softly and passionately. Greg, who was down the other end of the bed, slowly ran his hands up and down her stockinged legs, unclipping and sliding the stockings off, one leg at a time. Greg then slipped Chelsea's panties down her thighs and blew softly on her genitalia, she could feel his warm breath. John unclipped Chelsea's bra and released her bountiful breasts with erect nipples which were awaiting his touch. John slowly caressed Chelsea's breasts and sucked on her nipples, sucking them so hard that she flinched. Meanwhile Greg had parted Chelsea's legs and pushed her legs up so he could gain access. She was very moist and Greg softly licked Chelsea's swollen lips and erect clitoris, she groaned with pleasure. Greg was lying face down on the bed with his head between Chelsea's thighs, he was licking and sucking Chelsea's clitoris and pushing his fingers into her to watch the juices flow as he pulled them in and out. John straddled Chelsea's chest, he held both breasts tightly together and pushed his manhood between them after dribbling saliva down into her cleavage, it was gliding with ease as the saliva worked its magic. John was groaning with pleasure and Chelsea used her hands to massage his balls.

As John was thrusting in between her breasts feeling his balls been squeezed, he felt like he was in heaven. Chelsea was moaning in pleasure as Greg stretched her by using different numbers of fingers, this gave a completely different sensation each time he pushed his fingers in. Sometimes he just used one finger which glided effortlessly in and out, he could do this faster, then he pushed two fingers in which was tighter and he would go slower until she got used to it and stayed relaxed. He then tried three fingers, this induced pain and Chelsea cried out, Greg then eased his fingers ever so slowly to allow Chelsea to get use to the size and the stretching even dribbling saliva over his fingers to help ease the pain before slowly pushing in, very tenderly. Chelsea groaned with pleasure as she felt full to capacity and pressure as she was being stretched. John, at the top of the bed, pushed his manhood into Chelsea's mouth, she took it hungrily almost to try and distract herself from the sensations she was feeling below. Every time Greg pushed into her she would groan causing vibrations to reverberate along John's shaft, in turn this made him groan as her grip on his shaft would tighten each time her pleasure down there heightened.

John and Greg got up to change positions. John sat at the end of the bed and got Chelsea to sit backwards on him. As she lowered herself onto him, he could feel how hot and wet she was as he glided in with ease. Greg stood in front of Chelsea with his manhood rock hard and she took it into her mouth. She went up and down his shaft whilst massaging his balls with her hands. As John thrust into her she would groan, and now Greg could feel this vibrate up his shaft.

Greg suggested they use the sex swing. They helped Chelsea up and walked over to it. Both men lifted Chelsea into it which took her off the ground so that she was waist high to the men with her feet in each of the stirrups, legs splayed apart and hands holding the sides like a normal swing. Greg stood to the side of the swing and kissed Chelsea passionately but slowly to ensure her juices kept flowing. He caressed her breasts, pinching her nipples, to ensure it sent tingles throughout her body. John took his position at the front of the swing and held Chelsea's thighs underneath so that he could plunge deep into her. She let out a cry of pleasure as John thrust in and out, hard and fast.

The swing kept banging on the door with every thrust. Greg was so excited to watch the scene it kept him rock hard in anticipation for his turn.

John pulled out knowing if he continued he would cum and needed to restrain himself to make it last. Greg took over, moving Chelsea's legs up onto each shoulder to gain maximum depth inside her. Greg plunged into Chelsea who cried out and clenched her fingers onto the swing. John held her face in his hands lovingly to sooth her and kissed her softly. Greg pulled out and the men helped Chelsea out of the swing and they returned to the bed. Greg suggested that John lie on his back and Chelsea hover over him on all fours, her face above his manhood. Chelsea started to suck John slowly and glide her hand up and down his shaft. Meanwhile Greg mounted Chelsea from behind holding her hips in place pushing his member deep into her. Chelsea choked on a cry of pleasure and sucked tighter, each plunge inside her sent her face further down onto John's shaft. They were all groaning with pleasure at this point, as Chelsea sucked, and her pleasure increased with each thrust, she not only flowed with love juices but also had her saliva flowing all over John's manhood. Greg pulled out and dropped down to slurp up Chelsea's juices, each time he flicked her clitoris with his tongue it drove her wild sending more juices flowing.

The men decided to switch places again. Greg lay on the bed and Chelsea straddled him lowering herself down onto his throbbing member, sliding down its shaft and groaning with pleasure. To ensure John was still included in the action she put her legs around Greg's waist whilst he continued to thrust deep into her and she could lie down on her back as John stood at the end of the bed lowering his throbbing member into Chelsea's mouth. Upside down and facing up Chelsea took John's throbbing member deep into her throat, holding his hips and pulling him closer. As John thrust into Chelsea's mouth he continued caressing her breasts. She felt sensations all over, her womanhood, her breasts and her mouth, it was overwhelming. John loved the sensation on his throbbing member but was also enjoying the sight of Greg thrusting into her love nest, making her breasts bounce and they danced uncontrollably before him.

Chelsea released John's throbbing member and searched with her mouth for his swinging balls, she took them both into her mouth at once, filling her mouth, sucking on them and squeezing them, John was groaning with pleasure. Chelsea released them but kept the sack skin between her teeth, tugging it, which made John flinch. Chelsea put her finger into her mouth to lubricate it then pushed it behind John's balls until she found his cavity and pushed her finger into him, John yelled out with pleasure and she pushed in and out of him with her finger while taking his throbbing member back in her mouth, she sucked up and down to the same rhythm of fingering him. John was in ecstasy and was groaning really loudly. Chelsea knew he wasn't going to hold on much longer. She stopped and suggested they switch again. John said he was so close that he would sit in the chair and watch so he can last longer. Greg & Chelsea stood up and he bent her over making her touch her toes and he entered her from behind. Chelsea let out a big cry as he went so deep. Greg held onto her hips, thrusting hard and fast, Chelsea was crying out as Greg groaned louder and louder.

Greg stopped and pulled out knowing that he too was getting close. He got Chelsea to lie on the bed with her legs spread apart so he could kiss and lick her swollen lips and clitoris. Greg licked her as though he was mopping up spilt liquid, slurping her juices and swallowing them. Chelsea knew if Greg kept touching her clitoris she would soon explode. They all knew the time was nearing the crescendo and agreed it would be good for all three of them to cum at once. Greg wanted John to cum in Chelsea so suggested they decide on a position. John loves Chelsea riding him so decided he would lie on the bed whilst Chelsea straddled him. Chelsea then lowered herself onto John, effortlessly gliding down his shaft as she was so wet it eased the way. Chelsea started to ride John up and down and Greg stood alongside her so that she could take him into her mouth. Chelsea started to suck Greg as she bounced up and down on John's throbbing member before she started to rub her clit which was electrifying and making her tighten around John which heightened his excitement making him pump harder.

Chelsea being pumped harder bounced and her mouth pushed deeper onto Greg's shaft, she tightened her grip with her mouth by sucking harder. Chelsea started to rub her clit faster and could feel the pressure building, John was pumping harder and faster as Chelsea's juices flowed enabling him to go deeper. Greg was thrusting into Chelsea's mouth which was drooling more saliva as it went up and down the shaft. They could all feel the pressure building intensely and Chelsea starting to cry out first, long and hard, which excited the men to see her pleasure as her eyes rolled back in her head and her face grimaced with intensity. John was next shouting out, thrusting his last drops and jerking spasmodically. Greg too lost his load into Chelsea's mouth which she gulped, swallowing quickly to keep up with his flow, as some oozed out the corners of her mouth. They all were convulsing their last throes of pleasure until they all slumped into a heap drowned in sweat, cum and love juice. They felt spent and all three just lay on the bed to catch their breath. John said "wow", Greg replied "I reckon" and Chelsea said "that was awesome, we must do this again". They all laughed.